Girl at the back.

Copyright © 2017 Kat Green
All rights reserved.

DEDICATION

This book is dedicated to my amazing family and friends who have supported me. Also, to the bands who provide some incredible music that never fails to inspire me.

1

I looked at the ticket in my hand and smiled. After waiting for so long this night was finally here and I felt excited but a little nervous. I checked myself in the mirror; tight black jeans and my band T-shirt to blend into the crowd. My black curls, which had taken an hour to do, hung loosely down my back. And my emerald bracelet that matched my eyes to complete my outfit.

After a bus journey into town, grabbing a pack of cigarettes on the way, I arrived at the venue. I usually tried not to smoke but, on a night, out it was OK. A social smoker was my thing, smoke at the weekend and pretend that being smoke-free during the week was somehow healthier. It was deceiving myself but was a habit I'd failed to break with the odd one creeping in when work stressed me out. I certainly needed one this evening.

The venue appeared in front of me, the letters standing out like a beacon. That night's headline band, Contact Insanity, were causing quite a stir.

I joined the line and checked my phone. Nothing exciting to report via social media, just the usual posts – people complaining about their bad day, political issues or their dinner. I would broadcast my evening plans to the world if I could. But not having that luxury I didn't bother. It would all be lies anyway. I just blended in with the crowd and tried to act like I was waiting for someone.

There was excited chatter all around me as people continued to join the line, mostly girls all made up just in case they were lucky and met the band or a crew member. It didn't matter who as long as they could say they'd met so and so, or maybe they'd catch the eye of a band member which was possible if you were lucky. I was living proof that anything can happen when you least expect it. It was hard to keep a low profile but that was what I had to do, how it had to be. I typed out a message on my phone and smiled smugly.

"I'm here, you got time for a little catch up? xx"

Ten minutes passed before my phone vibrated in my pocket.

"Is it cold outside?" He asked.

"Yes, it's fucking freezing. How long before you grace me with your presence?"

"When Shane releases my chains. Just sorting a few last-minute set details then meet me round the back. Blue door, be there in 10. xx"

I smoked another cigarette to pass a few minutes, made small talk with a few people then prepared to leave. It felt like forever since I had seen him, but it was only three months. Three months too long. I felt the butterflies in my stomach and smiled at the thought.

Suddenly, my night took a turn for the worse. I saw the car pull up and my heart sank as the beautiful model stepped out of the car all smiles and designer clothes. She looked flawless and my confidence dipped. I seethed as she walked past the excited crowd, stopping for autographs and photos before she looked at me, knowingly, awkwardly, before walking with ease through the stage door. We didn't speak. She knew who I was and there was no need for a discussion.

'I can't believe his girlfriend's here. She's so perfect and they're the perfect couple,' someone said behind me. I didn't turn round but looked at the floor and tried to hold back the tears. My plans had suddenly been shattered. I felt like screaming at them all. Instead, I looked at the floor and counted to ten.

My phone vibrated. "I'm so sorry. I didn't know she was coming. I swear!"

I tried not to be angry with him. He couldn't do anything about it because when he'd signed that contract he'd agreed to certain obligations. That was before he met me, and he's stuck with it. I delayed my response and he messaged again.

"Don't go, please. I need to see you."

My excitement had turned to disappointment and seeing him would only make it worse. I would get a small amount of time before he would have to pretend to be with her.

I left the excited fans and casually made my way round the back as planned. The tour bus came into view, black and gold, massive and spectacular. My heart hammered in my chest. The question tearing at me was should I continue with this madness or go home. I waited by the blue door, a private exit where he would soon walk through. The sound behind me was familiar and I didn't have time to turn around before I was picked up around the waist and lifted inside the bus and the door closed behind us. His lips were on my neck before I saw him. His voice calmed me.

'I'm so sorry. I missed you,' he

breathed in my ear.

I turned and our eyes met for a second before his kisses stopped any conversation. I pulled away after a minute and looked up at him, his eyes a sensuous chocolate colour, and his scruffy brown hair that looked messy but amazing all at the same time.

'Is that all I get tonight?' I asked. He looked torn and exhausted as he lit a joint. The smell of the cannabis was strong, and he let out a dramatic cloud of smoke. Robbie didn't touch anything else other than alcohol. Another myth that he'd cleared up. He'd done stuff in the past; he wasn't a saint. His band mates dabbled now and again. They could get whatever they wanted by clicking their fingers, but the novelty had worn off over the years. He had told me at the start of their rise to fame that he was regularly off his face because it seemed the thing to do, but it had started to damage his performance. He began to get lazy, couldn't be bothered and after a stern talk with their manager, Shane, he'd cleaned up his act.

'I told them I didn't want her here tonight. But promoting her latest perfume has become more important. I bet the money being exchanged sealed the deal. I can't stand this anymore,' he complained as he took another drag of the joint.

I couldn't stay angry with him. 'She is stunning,' I said feeling a bit down at her mere presence.

'Not to me she isn't,' he reassured me. But his voice was low, and he looked concerned. He knew how hard this was for me, that sometimes it made me feel like crap.

'It's OK,' I whispered.

'No, it isn't. I didn't expect it to be so hard. Stealing kisses with you, my girlfriend. It's like we're cheating, and we aren't.'

Robbie had been my secret for months after meeting him outside a gig. I'd thought that a chat and a photo was all that would happen, they weren't even my sort of band. It was Annie, my best friend, who had campaigned to go. I only knew three songs and the excitement about meeting them wasn't such an issue for me. Annie loved to hang around waiting for bands. She thought that was the best part. The thrill of not knowing if you'd get lucky. Annie wasn't a crazy stalker though. She was cool and knew where to wait and how to act.

That night we'd waited for hours and had just about given up when the doors opened, and Robbie appeared. A fag hung from his mouth and a lighter in his hand ready to light it as soon as he was in the open. Annie had confidently walked towards him and began chatting as if she'd known him for years. I stood beside her feeling awkward until he had turned his attention on me. I remember his smile and the smell of his aftershave. He had clearly freshened up. He had a different shirt on from the one he'd worn on stage. It struck me then that this was the guy I'd seen on TV, heard on the radio from time to time.

Annie says she picked up on his

vibe straight away and that's why she'd insisted on getting a photo of us both. A photo that had hit Instagram seconds later. The caption was "My Bestie and her future boyfriend." With a hashtag of "#Sexual tension at its peak".

'As if...' I mouthed at her. Everyone knew he was dating Kasha Woods. I had laughed at the thought but had to admit to being mildly disappointed that there was no chance. Standing next to him I could see the fuss about him. He was gorgeous, even better up close.

Several fans gathered and he dutifully did his thing quite happily, but he would occasionally look back at me as if checking I was still there. The rest of his band joined him, and I watched as they mingled with wide-eyed fans until their manager made some excuse and said they had to go.

As they headed towards the bus Robbie had whispered something in his manager's ear. Shane had looked at me and said something back. I didn't think anything of it. Shane had looked thoughtful but also slightly worried then he nodded. Then as he passed me, he leaned in and whispered, 'Got time for a drink?'

I thought this was just the usual rock star behavior and was ready to say no. Annie had other ideas and before I knew it we were on the tour bus. Drinks were handed out and Annie asked them so many questions that Rich their drummer asked if they should charge for this interview. Kasha was in Paris for a fashion show so hadn't been around that night. I had asked where his girlfriend was and the looks between him and his band mates were hard to miss. When he had told us the secret, that their relationship was all for show, and we had picked our chins up from the floor, Sammy, the band's bassist, moved to sit next to me while Robbie got off the bus to make a phone call.

'You know, he's never told anyone he didn't trust about that. He likes you.'

I had laughed loudly, nervously. Sammy hadn't been joking and he didn't laugh with me.

He carried on. 'I've been touring with him for years. I know when he likes someone.' He winked as Robbie reappeared and moved so he could sit next to me.

Then they had even dropped us close to home. It had been right out of their way, but Robbie had insisted much to his manager's annoyance.

Robbie had asked for my number and things went from there. He had been completely honest about how things would be at first, but he always had a way to make me secure even when it was difficult. Robbie also wanted to protect me from the public eye as he knew they would be ruthless towards me. They seemed to love to hate him, but I knew the real him and he was nothing like what they printed about him.

His band was building a reputation for being the bad boys of Indie bands. In truth, they were just normal twenty-something guys having fun. They might party hard, but they meant no harm and they always looked after me. The rest of the band were aware of our situation and helped as much as they could. Sammy had said that having a happy, chilled Robbie was best for all concerned. He could be quite moody if things didn't go his way. It was his band, which was something he reminded them all on a regular basis. He was in charge, or so he liked to think, but I had seen the bored looks whenever it got mentioned, usually when he was drunk. They were very cunning in getting us together knowing how little time we had, but they could only do so much.

Shane was OK, but if he was honest, he would admit I was a hassle he could do without. But he treated me fairly. He understood it was hard for me and I knew how important it was, for now, to keep quiet.

I didn't cause problems as that just made Robbie's life more difficult. Being the possessive girlfriend just wasn't in my nature. So far, we had been very careful and that kept things running smoothly.

And now, here I was with Robbie, his girlfriend, but his secret girlfriend, as he opened the fridge and pulled out two beers, handing me one.

'How's the tour going?' I asked, trying to avoid the awkward silence that was threatening to join the party. He smiled and gave me the rundown of funny events. My question worked, and in no time we were laughing hysterically. He held onto my hand the whole time as he talked, and it made me feel better. Just being in the same country was nice, being with him and knowing it wasn't a dream. Sometimes, a lot of the time, I would almost convince myself I'd imagined it.

'Oh, nearly forgot. I have your birthday present.'

'You remembered!' I thought with his hectic lifestyle it might have slipped his mind. My birthday had been the previous week, so it impressed me he'd had the time.

'Of course, I did. I'm not a dick.'

He left for a second and I heard him searching through bags. He came back with a red gift bag. Inside were three small beautifully wrapped packages, which clearly, he hadn't done himself. I opened them carefully. It seemed like a crime to rip the wrapping. The first was my favourite perfume, Gucci Rush, also Robbie loved it..

The second was a Tiffany charm bracelet. I had wanted one for ages, and he'd also put three charms on to start it off. A heart, a cat – I'm mad about cats – and a guitar.

'The heart is mine; I'm giving it to you. The cat is because you're a mad cat lady and the guitar represents me.' He was clearly proud of his choice.

I was very happy too and screamed as I saw the last present. It was a new iPhone 7. 'Robbie, these are amazing.'

He told me that the phone was already set up so there was no need to worry about the monthly charges as he was paying for it.

'Are you serious? I can't ask you to do that.'

'Yes, I'm serious. You're not asking me to do anything. I've decided to do it because I want to. Your phone is shit, and you needed an upgrade.'

It was true. My battery was on its last legs. I would charge it fully and within a few hours it was dead, which wasn't ideal when you have a boyfriend thousands of miles away. Nothing more annoying than being out and he calls and the phones dies.

'I'll have to transfer everything over tomorrow. And I need a new case and accessories. Oh, I can't wait. Thank you so much.' I grabbed him, kissing him. 'My presents are perfect.' I braved the next question that burned inside. 'So, tonight, will I see you or does the presence of Kasha Woods ruin that?'

'Yes, just might be a bit later than planned. Head back to my room once the gig's over and I'll be there. I just can't say what time for sure. Kasha isn't as bad as you think. She's alright and she's no threat to you. She wrapped your presents because my attempt was shocking. She said I couldn't give them to you looking like that.'

It angered me a bit that she had been involved but I let it go. It was a nice thing to do. 'Tell her thanks, she did a good job.' It was all I could say, even if it was through gritted teeth.

He kissed my lips softly and got up. 'I'll see you later, I promise.' He had to go – I knew the drill.

The buzz from his pocket confirmed my thoughts. The Robbie Hale search party was out. He pushed a hotel room key into my hand. 'Room 501,' he said.

I nodded, grabbed my coat and presents and quickly left the bus. It looked safe, with nobody about, so I couldn't be seen sneaking away from my own boyfriend. But as I rounded the corner and was passing a door, it opened and a hand grabbed my arm and pulled me inside. My mouth dropped open. Kasha Woods shut the door behind me, looking nervously over her shoulder to make sure nobody was listening.

'Leah, sorry. I didn't mean to startle you. I think it's time we talked,' Kasha said leaving me momentarily speechless. This had never happened before, and also her attitude was different. 'Please, I'm not your enemy. I need your help.'

'What?' I was really confused now.

You really must hate me. God, I would hate me too if I was in your shoes. But I just wanted you to know, I hate this too.'

I took a step back and cleared my thoughts. 'Er, OK.'

'He loves you; he talks about you all the time. He's never actually said it to me. He doesn't need to; I can see it in his eyes when he mentions you.'

This was getting weird, and I wasn't sure how to respond. My boyfriend's fake girlfriend seemed to want my approval. 'You said you needed my help?'

'Yeah, I do. I want you to...'

Kasha never finished her sentence. Her agent appeared and didn't seem impressed to see me with her client. 'Kasha, what are you doing with her? Are you stupid?'

I watched Kasha being marched away, then she turned and looked back at me. She looked so sad and my heart dropped as I realised in that moment that she was unhappy. Something was wrong, but how could she be unhappy? She was one of the top fashion models, with bags of money and fame. I'd kill for a life like hers. Maybe she was selfish and seeking more. Gigi, her agent, came back and marched towards me. She looked furious.

'What are you playing at? You cannot be in here. Stay away from Kasha. While she is here you cannot be anywhere near Robbie. Stupid girl. You will ruin everything,' Gigi warned me then turned on her heels and strutted off. Once I'd recovered from her outburst, everything I wanted to say, and should have said, came to mind. I had been too shocked at the time. How dare she talk to me like that? Words couldn't describe my anger at her. If that was how Gigi treated people, no wonder her client was unhappy. She had spoken to Kasha like dirt. I left before I could run after her and cause a scene.

The doors had now opened and the line was disappearing inside the venue. It was time to get a drink. I endured the ticket checking, the massive wait at the bar and finally found a spot at the back. It filled up quickly and eventually the support came on. I had no idea of their name or really took that much notice of them. My run in with Gigi still had me seething.

***

A whole bottle of wine had been drunk when Robbie and the band finally took to the stage and I roared along with the crowd, singing every word. I forgot about Gigi and enjoyed the show, just the girl at the back, and just like everyone else as far as they knew. If only they knew the truth.

Once they were nearing the end

of their final song I left and went outside. The cold air hit my face making me stumble a little. I was more drunk than I thought and had to steady myself against the wall to compose myself. The whole bottle of wine and hardly any food that day was not sitting well. I got myself together and walked towards the hotel which was only a short way up the street.

    I decided to send Robbie a seductive text, but as I hit the send button someone pushed me from behind and I fell to the floor, dazed for a few seconds. My phone was ripped from my hand and then my attacker was gone.

    'No!' I screamed. 'Help me, someone.'

2

My heart was pounding as panic began to take hold. It wasn't because someone had attacked me but the phone, and what was on it. I staggered to my feet and ran to the hotel, taking the lift and running for Robbie's room. Once inside I searched his room trying to find his laptop, anything to contact him. It was awful how these days if you didn't have a mobile phone, you felt completely disconnected from the world.

His iPad was tucked under a pile of clothes left dumped in a corner. I had never worried too much about losing my phone before but now I had so much to protect. If they searched my phone they would know everything. Our private conversations, photos, the lie about Kasha. There was a way to block your phone and erase it but I couldn't think straight. I couldn't remember any of my log in details. My mind was blank.

It was only after I had calmed a little and looked in the mirror that I was aware of the pain. There were only minor cuts to my hands and legs, but the bruises were already forming.

Robbie had to know that my phone was gone and that potentially our secret could be out. The only way was to send a message through Twitter, privately. Once that was done, I cleaned myself up and poured another drink. Suddenly, I had sobered up and now needed something to calm my nerves.

I took my vodka and coke and stepped out onto the balcony, lit a cigarette with shaking hands and thought about what had happened. My new phone was safe as my bag hadn't been touched. But it didn't stop all my private information being in the hands of a stranger. I should have transferred everything over sooner. Everything had been lost. My phone had been taken while I was halfway through a message. It would have been unlocked, and I threw up at the thought of it. An hour passed before Robbie raced into the room, finding me in the bathroom crying my eyes out.

'Babe, are you OK?' He grabbed hold of me and checked me over.

I assured him I was fine, just a bit shaken up. 'I'm sorry, my phone... it's gone. It has everything on it...' My words came tumbling out in my panic.

'Leah, I don't give a shit about the phone. I'm just glad you weren't seriously hurt. Let me worry about the phone if there is a need to. Hopefully, they'll be more interested in wiping it to sell on. Did you see their face?'

I shook my head. It had happened so fast I only saw the back of them as they ran off.

'Do we call the police?' I asked.

'Do you want to?' Robbie asked.

'No. It would just create awkward questions. The phone has gone and no chance I'm getting it back. I've tried to block it but my mind was blank...'

Robbie held me tightly. 'Use my phone and call the phone company. I'm sure they can help. It'll be fine. If anything does come out, my PR people will deal with it. Don't worry.'

I moved away from him and threw myself on the bed, screaming into the pillow. I had been mugged and the person would get away with it because I was too scared to report it. Anything could blow our secret wide open, which would put Robbie in a difficult position. Suddenly, his arms were around me and he pulled me up, holding me tight until I had calmed down.

'I'm so pissed off. I'm drinking and hanging out with her, and you're being mugged. I didn't see your message at first. Fuck!' I could hear the anger and frustration in his tone.

I wiped my tears away. 'This isn't your fault. I went into this knowing how it would be. I'm doing it because I love you. You gave me a choice and I chose to be with you no matter what. But I'm struggling, Rob. I'm a burden you don't need. I ...' I trailed off, unable to say it, didn't want to say it.

Robbie stared at me. He picked up on my vibe, knowing what I was thinking. 'Don't say it.' He sounded angry.

'It can't work. I'm just an inconvenience to you, to everyone.' I struggled from his grip and picked up my bag, but he stopped me.

'You are not an inconvenience. Fucking hell, you can inconvenience me as much as you like. I love you. They stick a model on my arm day in, day out but all I think about is you.' Robbie pulled me closer. 'Don't say it, Leah, please.'

'Just lie with me,' I said instead. Robbie nodded and we lay in silence. I needed time to think but having his arms around me wasn't making it easy. Later, I watched as he frantically typed into his phone. He conversed with whoever it was for a while before throwing the phone on the floor.

'What are you thinking?' he finally asked, breaking the silence.

I knew what I should do, what the obvious outcome would be, but could I walk away from him? It was a hard decision to make. He was looking at me in that way, the one that stopped my heart. I wish he wouldn't do that tonight, not when I'm trying to sort out my next step. No, it was too late for making decisions. I grabbed him, kissed him, and pulled him towards me. We had one night, and I was going to make the most of it. I jumped off the bed and emptied the fridge of every drink they had and threw it all on the bed.

Robbie looked up at me, and his smile was wicked. His phone kept ringing, but he ignored it. He was supposed to be seen leaving with Kasha and going to some party but it seemed he wasn't playing by the rules tonight.

'Fuck it. Let's party,' he shouted as I opened the first bottle and jumped on him. His hands grabbed my waist pulling me against him. His phone starting ringing again.

'You should go, Kasha's waiting.' I

spat the words out.

Robbie pulled my face down to his.' She'll be waiting a long time.' He smiled that wicked smile again as he quickly pulled my top off. My mind was cleared of any thought of walking away as his kisses trailed over my breasts. Damn you, Robbie Hale.

***

As I opened my eyes the hangover hit me. My head was throbbing as I sat up, laughing even though it hurt. The room was an utter mess. Clothes had been thrown everywhere and empty bottles littered the room. Robbie's phone was ringing again but he was not moving anytime soon. He was still in a deep sleep, and he looked peaceful. The phone rang, and assuming it would be Shane I answered and waited for the barrage of insults. But it wasn't Shane.

'Leah, can you put him down. Shane is not happy. Robbie is not popular this morning. Tell him he has about eight minutes before he's dragged out.' Sammy, the band's bassist laughed before asking if I was OK.

'I'm fine. Pissed off, phoneless and hung-over, but alive.' We chatted for a bit, and then I suddenly thought about the previous night. 'Sam, look after him. He might need you to keep him grounded.'

There was silence from the other end for a few seconds. 'Leah, what are you talking about?'

'Just promise me, Sam.'

Sammy promised, but he knew what I wasn't saying. He didn't have time to discuss it and told me to get Robbie up, then he told me the time.

'What! Oh shit. He's getting up.' I shook Robbie awake, which didn't please him and resulted in a barrage of profanities. It was 10.55 and he could add being late to his list of things his manager would be pissed with him for. I watched, laughing, as he threw his belongings into his bags and half-heartedly washed in record time. He threw his stuff out the door ready to go then walked over to me, looking a little sad.

'That wasn't the goodbye I had in mind. Take care of yourself and I will fix this. I don't know how or when but I will.' He kissed me and I kissed him back fiercely, knowing it was to be our last. A minute later he was gone.

I sat for a long time just staring at the mess we'd made before I let my sadness go. Once all my tears had fallen for what felt like an eternity, I got cleaned up and left with a heavy heart.

The journey felt long, leaving me exhausted when I finally got home. The shower felt good and would hopefully wash away what had happened. The small bruises and cuts confirmed that nothing had changed. With no plans to go anywhere for the rest of the weekend, I threw on my pajamas and spent an hour playing with my new phone and feeling guilty and confused. When Robbie called, the conversation couldn't wait any longer. Sammy had told him about what I had said.

'What did you mean, look after me?' he asked sounding nervous.

I couldn't find the words, but my silence was enough. 'I don't know what I want. Last night shook me up. Kasha makes me feel crap, actually.'

He sighed and the sound seemed to echo in my ear. 'She's nothing to me. How many times do I have to tell you that?' Robbie snapped.

I explained that it wasn't anything he did. 'It just sucks having to be in the shadows. I want to be on your arm, proud to be by your side.' Robbie let me get everything off my chest. 'I just need a bit of space. I'll call you in a few days.'

I didn't let him respond before hanging up. My weekend was just getting worse. I decided the best thing to do was crawl into bed and sleep until Monday. I'd get up for work and only that. Maybe.

I slept most of the day and had fully immersed myself in Season 4 of *The Vampire Diaries* to forget about Robbie Hale. Unfortunately, not even Damon Salvatore could help me on this one. I wasn't sure if I could go through with my plan and decided that staying in bed was the best plan.

3

Monday morning arrived quicker then I wanted, and the rain didn't help my mood. I was already late but was in no rush to get there. After sitting in traffic for thirty minutes I finally made it to my desk and prepared for a day of listening to people moan about every little thing. My job for a retail company was on the customer service side. Nothing worse than being late and soaked through, and that was just walking from the car park. Thankfully, my boss wasn't there to see my dramatic arrival.

Kelly, my workmate, and company gossip, laughed as I sat down. 'What happened to you? Did you fight waves on the way in?'

'Yeah, it's vile out there.'

Kelly jumped up and did the tea round. She handed me my mug and I cupped it with both hands and held it to my face. 'God, I'm cold,' I complained while waiting for my computer to spring to life.

Having dried myself as much as I could, and after several sips of tea, I started my day. Luck was with me as Kelly informed me that the boss was also running late. There was the usual chatter of what everyone had been up to over the weekend, and I lied and said I'd been ill, so hadn't been out.

'You do look a bit run down.' Kelly looked concerned. 'In fact, you've not been yourself for a while now. Everything OK?'

I fobbed her off with some lame excuses but assured her I was fine. She did a check of the office and smiled when the threat of management wasn't evident. It was her chance to check her social media and the latest gossip. I took my first call and pretended to care about a parcel that hadn't arrived. As I hung up Kelly began laughing.

'No way,' she said, her voice a high pitched shrill.

She looked at me and I knew she'd got gossip. 'OK, spill.' There was no way she'd be able to keep it from me.

'You're a fan of Contact Insanity, right?'

I felt my stomach knot but played my poker face. 'They're OK.'

'Well, it seems Robbie Hale has been a naughty boy.'

A few others were coming over to have a nose as I slowly walked towards Kelly's desk, not knowing what would confront me. But I had to keep up my act. I saw the article and bile rose in my throat.

"Robbie Hale: Cheats on Kasha" was the headline on every gossip site. That wasn't the worst of it. Screen shots of messages from my stolen phone were there as evidence. My only saving grace was that my name hadn't been revealed. It had been blurred out. The girls in the office continued to dissect the article, but everything around me became fuzzy. Then all went black.

***

Kelly helped me into my flat and fussed around me until I finally convinced her she could go. After my embarrassing fainting episode, the only good thing was being sent home. Kelly had offered to drive me to make sure I was OK.

'Call me if you need anything,' she said as she left.

I let out a sigh of relief, at finding myself able to fall to pieces in private, which I did for an hour until my face hurt from crying. Everything had gone so wrong in one weekend. My phone, which had been in my bag, was still set to silent. There were sixteen missed calls, mostly Robbie and a few from Annie. I had to speak to him, so I called him back.

'Leah, are you OK?'

'No, Robbie, no. I'm not OK. I'm sorry.'

'Stop!' Robbie yelled. 'This isn't your fault. Come and see me. I need to see you. I'll send a car. Please.'

It seemed a ridiculous idea to me. 'Is that wise?'

'I don't care right now. I don't

care about anyone else but us.'

'What do we do?' I asked.

'Let me worry about that. I'll fix it. My people will fix it.'

That was the moment I knew dating him could never be simple. It would never be a normal relationship. 'That's the point. I don't want your people to fix things. I want us to fix things together. We cannot be an ordinary couple. I thought I could do this but I'm not sure anymore.'

Robbie sighed heavily. 'I can't argue with that. You're right. But one thing's certain and that's I love you.'

'I know. I love you too, Robbie. But I'm so confused.'

Robbie suggested me going to him again. 'Please. Let's talk this through, face to face. If you are going to walk away from me I want to at least see you one last time,' he pleaded.

It was only fair that we did this face to face. We needed closure. I was about to break his heart and my own. This couldn't work. Robbie would have to be extra careful now which is why I thought it was a ridiculous idea. But soon it wouldn't matter anymore.

***

The numbers flashed on the lift screen as I made my way up to the Robbie's floor. Seeing him wouldn't help me one bit and my mind raged a war with my heart. The door opened before I had even knocked and I melted in that moment as I took in his hair, his eyes. The only thing missing was his smile. He looked stressed and that worried me. He pulled me inside and slammed the door shut.

'What's happened now?' I asked, dreading his answer.

'Things are fucked up. I'm needed tonight, to be seen with Kasha acting like we're fine.'

It wasn't a new thing so his reaction seemed a bit off. 'And...'

'You've not heard the best bit.' He laughed but not in an amused way. 'They want her to wear an engagement ring.'

My mouth dropped open, and my heart shattered. 'No. No,' I yelled. Robbie grabbed my hands and pulled me against him. 'That is too much. No, Robbie.'

'I've said no. Kasha doesn't want this either, but apparently, it's a must. Damage control.'

I was livid and it wasn't because I felt it for me, not completely. The lack of compassion for Robbie and Kasha astounded me. 'This is unfair on you. When you decide that marriage is what you want, you should have the right to choose who and when it happens. You're not an object. What's next? An actual wedding? Will you have to marry her to keep these pricks happy?'

He smiled at that. 'There's the reason why I love you. Your compassion for others. If anyone should be wearing a ring, it isn't Kasha. There is no way I will marry her. That is where I draw the line.' He stroked my cheek. 'There's only one woman who'll be my wife and she's about to walk away from me.' He kissed me on the forehead. 'I've got to go and meet Shane, band meeting, and then I've got an interview.' He knew he would be asked about the latest scandal.

'What will you say about it.'

'I'll deny it. It was fake and me and Kasha are fine, blah blah.' He looked bored at the thought of it all. 'Kasha will be somewhere else having the same conversation. It's all so fucking boring. I'll be back after the gig.'

I let him go and promised to stay to talk later. If this was the end of us, then things were not going to be left unsaid. I tried to read my book but couldn't concentrate, so I got a drink from the mini bar and flicked through the channels on the TV. The usual shows bored me within minutes. Refreshed by a shower I curled up on the bed and sleep took over till a knocking at the door woke me. It was gentle and seemed as if whoever it was didn't want to be heard. I jumped up and checked the peep hole and my mouth dropped open. It took me a few seconds to compose myself before opening the door. Kasha stood awkwardly as she looked around her nervously.

'Leah, please let me in. I need to talk to you.' I stepped aside and she rushed into the room. 'Shut the door quick,' she begged.

I slammed the door shut feeling irritated. As if I didn't feel bad enough, here stood Kasha Woods, stunning model. Her perfect blonde hair, flawless looks and designer clothes and my boyfriend's fake girlfriend.

She sat on the bed and kicked off her expensive shoes and sighed with relief. 'That's better. I've wanted these off all morning, they kill.'

My anger erupted in sarcasm. 'Oh, are they not good enough, not expensive enough? I have a spare pair of shoes, maybe you'd like to take them from me too.' My whole body was shaking with anger. Kasha looked up at me and her response was unexpected. She fell to pieces; her sobbing was heart-wrenching.

'I'm so sorry… I shouldn't have bothered you.' She picked up her shoes and walked towards the door. 'I–I just needed somewhere to go to be me, just for a minute.'

I felt horrible. I'd been so wound up over Robbie I hadn't even noticed how sad she'd looked when she'd turned up. 'Wait. Kasha, stay. You're right we do need to talk.'

Kasha smiled and dropped the shoes. 'The shoes are beautiful, but they hurt me and to be honest I want to wear something comfy just for a change. I'm not ungrateful but they aren't even mine. I'm paid to wear them.' She wiped the tears from her face. I grabbed her some tissue and offered her a drink.

'No, thank you. I'm scheduled for a shoot tomorrow.' My expression must have shown my confusion. 'I can only eat or drink certain things before a shoot.'

'Bollocks,' I snapped. 'There's nothing to you.'

'Yeah, that's why I'm in modelling.'

She sat down on the bed again, looking miserable, and I wanted to know more about her. I sat down next to her and decided to give her a chance to talk. She wiped more tears away.

'I know how bad this must make you feel,' she said finally. 'I hate it. Robbie hates it. It was fine in the beginning, fun even. Then he met you and it changed everything. I care about him, as a friend and that's all. I want you to know that. There has never been anything romantic between us, never.' She explained that what was printed in the press was it. 'Before you, he would never settle with just one. I saw the girls throw themselves at him. He'd indulge sometimes if he was in the mood.'

I knew all this; it wasn't a secret.

'Then you came along, and you were different. I asked him once what made you stand out from the crowd. He said you were special because you didn't drop your knickers or treat him like he was a star. He respected that. He said you made him work for it. He knew you were the one. That he knew you loved him for himself and not because of what he did.'

I smiled at Kasha, warming to her a little. 'That's nice to hear. Thanks.'

'It's OK. I just wanted you to know I'm not a threat. I've no intention of getting with him, I never have. We help each other cope with this madness. I'm in love with someone else...'

I snapped to attention at this. 'You asked for my help. Is this why?'

Kasha nodded. 'He doesn't even know it. I want him to, but it's never going to happen. It can't ever happen.' Kasha looked lost. 'I guess I kind of know how you feel. The need to be with someone but knowing it can't ever be.'

I stood up, walked to the mini bar and flung the door open. It was filled with bottles of wine, spirits and beer, crisps and chocolate. I picked up a handful of chocolate bars and flung them on the bed, then grabbed several bottles of wine and two glasses.

'You are going to drink this wine and eat that chocolate,' I ordered.

Kasha stared longingly at the contraband. 'I'm so hungry,' she whispered.

I opened a chocolate bar and placed it in her hand. 'One fucking bar isn't going to make you fat. A glass of wine isn't either.'

Kasha devoured the chocolate in seconds then reached for another. Once she'd finished, she lay down on the bed, smiling. 'That was amazing.'

I poured the wine and handed her a glass. We toasted to being rebels then polished off several mini bottles.

'I think I'm getting tipsy,' she said, giggling.

Suddenly, it dawned on me that Kasha really wasn't a threat, in fact she was nice. I was starting to like her more with every passing minute. Her phone had been ringing the whole time she had been in the room and I asked who it was.

'Gigi.' She took a deep breath before continuing. 'Don't get me wrong. She's a fantastic agent and I do owe her a lot, but she doesn't let me breathe. Lately she has become hard to handle. She doesn't like you, Leah. She thinks you are going to ruin everything. I've told her that me and Robbie could just release a press statement saying we've split up. She went completely mental. I don't get what is so important.'

This shocked me. 'You would do that?'

'Yes. We both need to be free. If we just played the game and did the whole break up but were still friends act. Give it a month or two for the storm to settle and live a happy life.'

It was a perfect solution. 'You want to be free to seek out this guy you like?' I asked. Kasha's face fell and she shook her head. 'Why not? Is he married or something?' She shook her head again. I put my hand on her shoulder. 'You can trust me. Who is it?'

Kasha sighed heavily 'I can't ever

have him. It wouldn't look good if I split with Robbie then stepped out with one of his band mates.'

My mouth dropped open. 'Oh, shit. Who?'

'Sammy.'

I didn't see that coming and was speechless for a few seconds. Kasha had said his name with real fondness. 'Wow! Kasha, if he feels the same and Robbie just says he gives his blessing to the goddamn world, for sake of saving face, you should do it. Sammy is a great guy.'

'I'd be hated.'

'Who gives a fuck? The keyboard warriors will have their say for a week or so until they find something else to gossip about.' I knew part of me was thinking of how good this was for me, but another part of me wanted her to be happy too. 'Have you spoken to your friends? True friends will support you. My best friend always supports me.'

This opened up another revelation about Kasha and I suddenly felt really sorry for her.

'God, I envy you, Leah Marley. A man who loves you. and a best friend.'

'You don't have a best friend?'

Kasha shook her head. 'Not anymore. I sacrificed any true friendships for my career. I lost sight of what was important at the start. I was never around, always away too busy to answer my phone. It wasn't intentional. I didn't know how bad things had got and just took it for granted she'd always be around.'

I understood and thought I could help her get her friend back. 'Call her and tell her how sorry you are. If you were close, I'm sure you can fix it.'

Kasha burst into tears again. 'I would love to, but I can't.' Kasha explained that Polly had died three years ago. 'She'd left me several messages asking me to call. I'd been in LA working. The time difference made it difficult, my schedule was jam packed. After two days I finally had a few hours off, and it wouldn't have been too late in the UK. Polly's last message had me worried, she sounded so low. She was crying for me to call her. I ran back to my hotel to call her in private. I tried again next day but never got an answer. I thought she'd got fed up with me and was ignoring me. It turned out she'd been hit by a car and died a few hours later in hospital.

'Oh, Kasha. I'm so sorry. I–I don't know what to say.'

'She was the only person who was my true friend and I let her down. I should have made more of an effort. And I still don't know why she had sounded so upset when she'd called. I'll never know. And worst of all she died thinking I didn't give a shit.'

Kasha let it all pour out, the guilt over Polly, the loneliness. She had her entourage, but they were there for the perks. Once the cameras stopped flashing they were nowhere to be seen. She was put away until her next job.

'I know they're not my friends and it hurts. Gigi just bangs on about Robbie and how things look. It's driving me insane.'

'I think Gigi is a raging bitch,' I snapped. 'Yes. She's your agent but you can make your own decisions. This is utterly ridiculous. If you want to date Sammy, do that too. Gigi doesn't like me, but she is going to fucking despise me very soon. Let's show her you are not under her control.'

The wine had given Kasha confidence and she was easily convinced. I could see the power rise in her. The next few hours passed and we spoke about everything, laughed, and Kasha seemed more positive.

'Thanks, Leah. This has been the best few hours in a long time.' She had relaxed and had just demolished her third chocolate bar. 'Wow, that was good.' She downed more wine then grabbed a bottle of beer. 'Let's add more calories,' she said, giggling.

'I'm glad we've finally talked. It's been fun. You'll need to meet Annie.' I grabbed my phone and made a call. Bringing Annie up to speed she was up for the game.' I ended the call then checked the time. It was only 7:30 so there was plenty of time to get ready. I told Kasha to make herself comfy and drink more if she wanted while she waited.

'What are you doing?' Kasha asked, giggling again.

'We are going to the gig.' Robbie was due on stage just after 9 and we would be there. 'Annie will be here soon, and we are going to party.' Kasha raised her glass and cheered.

Less than an hour later Annie arrived. She marched in, her red-tipped brown hair flowing wildly. She was a few inches shorter than me even in heeled boots, but what she lacked in height she made up for in attitude. Annie didn't care too much about beauty, she was pretty in a natural way. She took care of herself, but her attitude was if you didn't like her natural, you could fuck off. She hardly ever wore dresses but could make a pair of skinny jeans and a vest top look stunning. That was her attire tonight, with black boots that could crush you if she decided to walk over you. Even the scar on her arm didn't bother her. When she was fifteen, she'd burned herself with an iron which had fallen off the ironing board onto her. It had landed hot side up. The dark scar was about three inches long and looked a bit like a diamond.

'I'm here.' She did a twirl as she entered the room. 'Right, so let me get this clear. Rob and Sammy are off the menu but the other two are single?' she asked, one eyebrow raised.

I laughed and told her 'All yours, babe.'

'Sweet, I want in on some rock star loving. See if it's worth it or just a bunch of crap. Most men can't handle me.' She roared with laughter and threw herself down next Kasha. She grabbed the bottle from Kasha's hand and downed the remaining contents. 'Sharing is caring,' she said and threw the bottle across the room. 'We are partying with rock stars, let's trash this room.'

I patted her shoulder. 'Annie let's

leave the trashing of hotel rooms. It's not really the thing these days.'

She looked disappointed. 'Boring,' she said with a yawn.

Kasha burst out laughing. 'I like you already.'

Annie turned, looking smug. 'I'm Marmite. You either love me or hate me. I don't give a shit either way but nice that you do. Anyway, let's get going.'

Kasha held her hands up. 'OK, but before we do, I think you need to be ready. We can't just walk out there and walk up like everyone else. I'm a celebrity. There'll be press, so on this part you need to follow my lead.'

Annie roared with laughter. 'Fuck them. Parasites. Kasha Woods is stepping out with her new besties and hangers on can stand outside. They are not getting the limelight this time.'

Annie took Kasha by the hand and dragged her out the door. I followed and prepared for the onslaught, but soon realised I was in no way ready for it

4

As we approached the venue the press surrounded us. Flashes blurred my vision and I was now in Kasha and Robbie's world. The girl from the hotel room was gone and the model had taken her place. She played it well, and no one could have told that underneath all the razzmatazz was a very lonely girl. She smiled and waved as the paparazzi continued to harass her. Until Annie took over.

'Listen, you've had enough pictures. She's not a circus act. Back off. What are you going to do next? Throw treats at her for playing well? We're here for a good night and you are not invited.'

I took hold of Kasha's arm and barged my way through the crowd, knocking a few cameras on the way. 'Yeah, back off. If any of you touch her, we will kick your asses,' I added looking fiercely into one camera. 'Her best mates are here tonight, and we don't like any of you.'

We were escorted though a side door and were soon backstage. Kasha leaned into me and whispered, 'Straight down the hall, turn left and it's the second door.'

I asked her what she meant and she smiled. 'Your boyfriend's dressing room. Go. He'll be in there.' My heart fluttered. This was the first time I had ever been backstage, and I couldn't help but feel a little excited by it.

The dressing room door opened and Vince, Robbie's guitarist, appeared. He pointed and looked around him mockingly. 'Security, we have a breach.' He laughed at his joke.

'But I just want an autograph. Please. I've travelled all day and everything,' I joked back.

Vince shook his head, his black hair pulled back into one of those short ponytails that didn't move. He walked over and hugged me tightly. 'You are breaking the rules,' he reminded me.

'I'm secretly dating a rock star. Rules are supposed to be broken,' I reminded him.

He laughed. 'True. I'm heartbroken. You are totally here for the singer.'

'Ah, Vince. Sorry, but you just won't do. Don't worry. There are plenty of others who'd happily take my place.'

Vince gave a fake cry before opening the dressing room door. 'I guess I'll have to make do.' He winked and let me past. 'Watch out! Gigi's on the warpath. Kasha's gone missing in action and she's not happy. The chain she securely fixes her to Robbie with clearly broke tonight.'

His lip curled up at the side. Vince loved winding Gigi up. He couldn't bear the woman, and unlike the others he didn't hide it. He would love what I had to say about Kasha's disappearing act, so I quickly brought him up to speed. He raised his hands in the air and looked absolutely delighted.

'Fucking brilliant. She's going to have a meltdown. I'm glad you two have cleared the air. She's alright, if

I'm honest. I thought she'd be a right stuck-up chick, but she's not and she hates all this too. I think Sammy might have a thing for her.' Vince had a look of a man whose mind was racing with the prospect of matchmaking.

'You're not interested?' I asked him.

Vince shook his head. 'No. She's cool, but I have my eye on someone else.' He winked again, and I remembered him talking about a girl once. Touring made it hard, but he held out hope she'd come around eventually. In the meantime, he'd enjoy himself. 'She'll give in one day. Anyway, I have a feeling our Sammy will be pleased with this news. He likes Kasha, and I won't get in his way.'

'Really?' I jumped excitedly and he looked at me questioningly. 'OK, spill, Marley.'

'Let's just say Gigi is going to hate me even more before tonight is out. Her client likes the bassist. She'll freak.'

Vince roared loudly. 'Yeah, let's play Cupid. Oh, this could be great.'

He grabbed my shoulders and it was obvious that a thought had just struck him. There might as well have been a light bulb above his head.

'If she hooks up with Sam then we could use this. You pretend to date him. No reason for you not to be with us, you and Robbie get more time together. And... Gigi gets a royal slap in the face.'

I patted his shoulder. 'I'll discuss it with Robbie.' I winked at him and went into the room.

Robbie had his back to me, his phone in his hand. I looked over his shoulder and read the message he was typing out to me. 'I'm fine.' He turned and nearly fell out of his chair. I pulled him upright and kissed him. 'I'm sorry, I'm not going anywhere.'

He kissed me again, then picked me up and sat me on the table. Then he locked the door. 'You wore a skirt. Good choice.'

'Robbie, we can't, not here,' I said, half serious. But on the other hand, I wasn't putting up much of a fight.

'The door's locked. We can tick doing it in the dressing room off the list.' He was already between my legs pulling my pants off. I didn't stop him. 'Just quickly,' he breathed in my ear. I nodded then his mouth covered mine.

***

|It wasn't romantic in any way, but I sighed with contentment when we'd finished. I never thought this would happen so it feels like a little victory. Now, fully dressed and the door unlocked we act like nothing happened as the room begins to fill up again. It wasn't until later that night that Robbie reveals to me that the others knew. It was what they did back at the start. If the door was locked it meant they'd got lucky and come back later. I felt mortified at first but then realised it didn't matter. Nobody made a big deal out of it, maybe because it wasn't a big deal to them.

I put my head on Robbie's lap and looked up at him. He was beautiful and he was mine. I told him about Kasha and what I'd discussed with Vince.

His eyes clouded over. 'This is going to make me sound like a hypocrite. I'm not sure...' He stopped and shook his head. 'Seeing you with Sammy.'

I sat up and glared at him. 'Are you fucking kidding me?'

Robbie held his hands up in surrender. 'I know I don't have any right to say no. Anyway, shouldn't Sammy be involved in this discussion before we agree to anything?'

The door swung open and Sammy filled the door frame. 'I'm in,' he said. He was grinning as he collapsed on the sofa next to me.

'So, Kasha likes me...huh...' He was looking very smug and had clearly heard every word of our conversation. 'Rob, dude, I think it's a great idea. It's not like I'm going to be shagging Leah or anything. Come on, think of the fun we could have with the press. We could make them look like utter fools. Plus, we could really wind Gigi up. She swans around our gigs like Lady Muck. Getting right on my tits.'

Robbie leaned back and closed his eyes. I looked at Sammy.

'He'll do it. Give him a minute,' he mouthed, then counted silently using his fingers.

At fifteen seconds Robbie sprung to life, his eyes wide. 'Fuck it. I'm in.' He too was sick of being controlled and Sammy had given him a good reason to be on board. Getting some control back. I hugged him tightly. 'You can be around me as much as you want.' He smiled and kissed my forehead.

'The sexual tension between those two is getting annoying. Go for it, mate.'

'Is it that obvious?'

'Sam, you might as well have a fucking banner.' Robbie laughed loudly.

'Shit. I thought I was playing it cool.'

'No way, mate.'

Sammy was punching the air just as Kasha entered the room. He leapt from the sofa and grabbing her arm pulled her to him, slamming the door shut. Kasha looked confused as Sammy ran his hands through her hair. 'I've been holding back far too long. Kasha Woods, will you go for a secret date with me, behind your fake boyfriend's back?'

Kasha looked at me then Robbie then back to Sammy. 'Is this serious?'

'I'm deadly serious.'

Kasha stepped forward so there was no space between them. 'I thought you'd never ask. I have expensive taste, so you'd better be prepared.'

Sammy laughed and hugged her. 'I've been prepared for months.'

Their moment was short lived as they were called to the stage. We watched from the side and I wondered where Annie had got to.

After several messages she finally arrived looking very pleased with herself. She leaned towards me. 'Sod

the band, I'm going for management.'
Before I could ask her to explain,
Shane appeared by her side and
handed her a drink. My mouth
dropped open but all Annie did was
mouth 'Watch this space'. I decided
to keep out of it. She was an adult
after all.

The gig was outstanding as usual,
with a girl somehow getting on stage
and almost knocking Robbie over, but
he dealt with it like a professional. He
stopped the security getting too
aggressive with her and even allowed
her to take a selfie before being
removed. Robbie loved the adulation
and liked to indulge now and again.
These fans were the reason they did
what they did, and he liked to
remember that. Some went too far at
times and he wasn't afraid to tell
them when he didn't appreciate it.

It had happened earlier that day
when a group of fans had seen them
heading inside the venue. The band
had stopped to spend some time with
them. One girl had her photo taken
with them all, and separately, but

then she wanted several things signed. It took a while which annoyed the other waiting fans. Then she asked Robbie if he'll call her friend and say hello. Shane had been tapping his watch impatiently, and Robbie had told the girl he wanted to give others a chance. He said no and the look on her face was disgust. She'd called him rude and burst into tears. Shane had moved them on. I was annoyed at the girl, because he wasn't rude. He was just trying to be fair on everyone.

Once they had left the stage and the crowd had left the building we made it to a bar backstage. The lads mingled with those lucky enough to be allowed access, promoters, press and music executives. Everyone seemed to have enjoyed the gig and the mood was good. It didn't last long once Gigi glided into the room.

'Kasha, Robbie, your car is outside. You have to head to Juliette's for drinks, be seen.' She clapped her hands like a school teacher. Juliette's was a new bar opening and they, for some reason, needed to show their faces at this high-class bar.

Robbie hated posh bars; he liked music venues, chilled out places. Juliette's was stuffy and too posh for his liking. Kasha looked just as thrilled as Robbie. I smiled at her and leaned forward. 'How about me and Sammy join you both?' I winked. Kasha perked up at my suggestion and took my hand. 'Leah and Sammy are coming too.'

Gigi looked murderous. Robbie laughed as he took Kasha's hand as they made their way to the door.

Sammy threw his arm around my shoulders, and I leaned into him. 'Come on, lover, let's party.'

Keeping the hysterical laughter under control was impossible as the press swarmed round us. Kasha couldn't even stand; she was completely hysterical. Shouts came at us from all angles.

'Kasha, have you forgiven Robbie?'

'Robbie, are you seeing someone

else?' At this we all roared again with laughter.

'Sammy, who's this? What's your name, love?'

Sammy was quick with a response 'It's my mum,' before dragging me inside the bar, where we were shown to a private table specially reserved.

'Are they always so intrusive?' I asked, still taking in my second experience of the paparazzi. It could be intense, and the reality was not something I liked.

'Yep, all the time!' Sammy said, a touch disdainfully. 'It's Catch 22. You need them but sometimes you just wish they would give you a moment to fucking breathe.' He put his arm around my shoulders and pulled me into him. It felt weird, and I saw Robbie grind his teeth and his hands balled into fists for a second and then he let it go. Kasha watched and I saw a look in her eyes, the one I guess my eyes showed too. Her hand in my boyfriend's hand made me start to think that this wasn't going to be as easy as we thought.

We stayed an hour and had a couple of drinks but once Robbie had decided they'd done enough he stood up. 'Let's go. It's boring as fuck. I'm out of here.'

It wasn't long before we were in the car and heading for the hotel. Outside, another pack had gathered.

'Fuck sake,' Robbie cursed. I could tell he was exhausted and looking forward to his day off. They had one day to rest before continuing with the tour. And I'd been promised his full attention, after a lie in.

'One last act for the night. Let's get inside,' Robbie ordered. He helped Kasha out of the car, putting his arm around her waist. She leaned her head on his chest acting tired as he moved them out of our way. 'Come on, give her some space. She's not feeling too good. She needs rest. Move!'

They were convincing, and I nearly believed it for a second. Sammy grabbed my hand and pulled me close to him. We weaved through them into the safety of the hotel lift and headed to the top floor. We dropped the hands we were holding and breathed sighs of relief.

'That was horrible. I can fully see how hard this has been on you,' Robbie apologised.

Sammy patted his shoulder. 'Are we good, man.' He seemed nervous as he asked.

Robbie nodded. 'Of course. Don't worry.'

We stopped at Robbie's door and watched Sammy head to his and Kasha to hers. Robbie coughed to get his band mate's attention. Sammy looked back and Robbie made a gesture with his head towards Kasha. It meant 'What you are doing, make your move'.

'Kasha, do you fancy a drink in my room?'

Kasha turned and without answering she linked her arm through his and they disappeared into his room. Robbie pushed me through his door and slammed it shut. 'Jesus, I've wanted to kiss you all night.' He pushed me down onto

the bed and that's where we stayed
until late next day

5

It took a while for it to register that the noise was my phone. I looked at the missed calls and the name of my boss sent my stomach flipping. Six missed calls meant she was not happy. I sat up and thought about the past few days. I'd been sent home and told to take a few days rest but then then go and parade around in front of a load of paparazzi. She must have seen it all. Then a text arrived.

'I wanted to discuss this with you face to face but you won't even answer the phone. So, hanging out with rock stars is way more important. I'm so disappointed, Leah. CALL ME ASAP!'

I felt sick and guilty. Donna had been a great boss and had always supported me in the years I'd worked for her. She had every right to be upset with me. I had to face this and soon.

Needing to wake up a little first, I got dressed and headed to the hotel restaurant. Thankfully it wasn't busy and there was an empty table in the corner away from everyone. A few businessmen tapped on laptops and several families battled with tired and hungry children. I was of no concern to these people.

Coffee and a croissant were all I could stomach. This was going to be an awful call and I panicked at the thought of losing my job. Tears were very near the surface. I should be happy but instead everything was a mess. My breakfast arrived and I took my time avoiding the call for as long as possible. The restaurant was empty when I had finished so taking a deep breath I headed back to our room.

'Leah, you're alive.' Her voice didn't have her usual warmth. It was harsh, sarcastic, and I felt even worse. 'I want the truth, all of it.'

She stayed silent as I told her everything, finally telling someone other than Annie my secret. 'I'm so sorry, Donna. I never meant to let you down. It's just a mess. But the fainting was true, and I was going to take a few days, but we thought everything was about to come out. I nearly ended things...' I wasn't sure if Donna was still there, it was so silent. But eventually she burst out laughing.

'Leah Marley, Jesus. I've had some excuses and explanations in my time but this one must be the best. So, let me get this straight. You are Robbie Hale's actual girlfriend?' I confirmed it again. 'Shut the fuck up. Leah, this is blowing my mind. Kasha Woods is fake?'

'Yes, they've never been romantically involved.'

'Wow. I should be majorly pissed with you. I am, but I have to say this is the best bit of gossip in years. Do you know how long I've been trying to get tickets to see them? It's impossible.'

This was news to me. Donna had never mentioned being a fan. 'If you don't fire me, I'll get you on the guest list.' It was a cheeky shot but if it worked it would be worth it.

'Are you trying to bribe me, Miss Marley.'

'No, yes. Please. I won't ever lie to you again.'

Donna thought for a second, and I heard her sigh. 'OK. Lucky for you I've not taken this to HR so I'll cover you this once. I want you back in work on Monday. Don't be late. If you don't turn up, that's it, no more chances. We'll chat then.'

I could have kissed her. I made her promise several times to keep my secret and she assured me she would. I hung up and turned to find Robbie staring up at me.

'Nicely handled. I take it you've saved your job.' His voice was hoarse, and he coughed. I noticed he was sweating.

'Are you OK?' I asked.

'I'll be fine. A strong coffee will sort me out.' He got up and headed to the bathroom.

I checked my phone for any other surprises and sent Annie a message to find out where she'd ended up. I hoped she'd headed home. It was wishful thinking.

"Bagged myself a tour manager. Chat in a bit babe. I'm a bit busy. X"

I let it go. She was an adult and who she dated wasn't my concern.

Robbie was coughing again, and he sounded awful. A few minutes later he returned to bed.

'Christ. I feel terrible, babe.'

I felt his forehead and he was red hot. 'You are sick. Get more sleep and see if you feel better later.' He nodded and was asleep instantly. Then I sent Annie a message telling her to let Shane know. It didn't take long before he was knocking at the door. He looked concerned as he came into the room.

'We need to be on the road shortly. How bad is he?'

'I'm not sure, but if Robbie says he feels awful then I guess that's exactly what he means. He never complains about being ill. I've seen him carry on when he's been sick before.'

'He looks like shit,' Shane commented. 'OK, I'll delay leaving for a few hours longer. Let me know as soon as he wakes up,' Shane said then left.

I lay next to Robbie and watched him till I fell asleep. He was still sleeping when I woke about an hour later, but he was paler and shivering violently. I put my hand on his face and he was freezing. I shook him to wake him, but he wasn't fully conscious.

'Robbie, babe. Robbie.'

'Everything hurts. I'm hurting,' he muttered. That's when I noticed the rash on his neck and arms. 'My neck…'

I jumped out of bed and grabbed a glass and pressed it against his skin. The rash didn't vanish like it would normally. He'd been saying he'd been feeling tired but had put it down to his lifestyle. I grabbed my phone and called Annie.

'Get an ambulance. He's sick.'

I tried to wake him up, but he was drowsy. He put his hands over his eyes as the sunlight was hurting them. I shut the curtains and covered him and held him as he muttered incoherently. Relief washed over me as Shane and Annie arrived and Shane took over.

'Ambulance is on its way, son. You're going to be fine.'

Annie put her arms around me. 'He's going to be fine,' she said, but I wasn't listening. He was covered with the rash and looked like he was dying. I couldn't stop the tears.

Ten minutes later the paramedics arrived, and he was taken to hospital. The next few hours seemed a blur with me being checked over too. In fact, everyone involved with Robbie had to be checked.

Robbie had viral meningitis. It was a relief as it was the less dangerous version, but it was still scary and needed immediate treatment. The doctor told me that my quick thinking had almost certainly saved him and prevented permanent damage, but we still needed to wait till he'd been seen properly to fully relax. The doctor was advising Shane on what Robbie would need going forward. At least two weeks rest and plenty of fluids. For now, he was being treated with intravenous antibiotics. Under no circumstances was Robbie to set foot on a stage, and he was to stay in one place if he was sent home. He had a severe case of the virus and would need to be fully recovered.

'He needs someone to stay with him until he gains his strength,' the doctor ordered.

'I won't leave his side,' I said without hesitation. That plan was short lived as Gigi appeared with Kasha in tow. Kasha was genuinely concerned for Robbie but the look she gave me was nothing short of sorry.

'Leah, I'm sorry but you need to leave. Kasha will take over now.'

I was left speechless, overcome with rage. But before I could respond Shane was in front of her. From his stance it was obvious he wasn't going to take her shit.

'Gigi, this is not the time or place for throwing your weight around. If you haven't got the memo, Robbie is seriously ill.' Gigi tried putting on a concerned face and trying to show she cared. Shane cut her off. 'No, shut up. I know you think this is a great way to further your client's career but not now!' he yelled. He gave me a sympathetic look. 'You will not throw Leah out. Kasha can stay but you can get lost.'

I had never thought Shane would stick up for me and it shocked me, but I was grateful. Gigi looked like she'd been slapped in the face. She was livid but Shane wasn't letting her control this moment, and he leaned into her face. 'Get out. Robbie would want Leah here. So back off.'

Gigi glared at him for a few seconds then walked out.

Kasha watched her go but didn't follow her. Once the door had closed, she ran to me and threw her arms around me. 'I am so sorry about this. I told her to leave it. How is he?' Kasha took Robbie's hand and kissed it. Shane filled her in on his condition and I saw her eyes fill with tears.

'Come on, Rob, you can fight this. We all need you.'

I was full of admiration for her. She cared for him, but it was obvious it wasn't romantic, more like a sister. She gently placed his hand back on the bed and crouched down in front of me.

'He'll be OK, I know it. Listen to me, he's like a brother to me and I'll do what I have to for press reasons. But when you want privacy all you have to do is say.'

I hadn't realised how hard I had been holding my emotions back, but they erupted suddenly and I cried heartbreaking sobs. 'I can't even be here for him like a proper girlfriend. I hate this.'

Shane put his hand on my shoulder and gave it a gentle squeeze. 'Leah, you've been amazing through all of this fucked up situation. You could have made my life and Robbie's difficult. You didn't. I'll admit I wasn't sure about you at first. These past few weeks you've proved to me that you love him, and I've seen him change with you. He's happier when you're around. That's why I gave G her marching orders.' I thanked him through sobs. 'No problem, babe. I feel better having you here. I can do what's needed knowing he's got you.'

The rest of the night was a blur as his band mates came to see him. Kasha made several appearances to the press to keep up the charade. Then when we had to leave, Sammy joined me to keep up the story. At least that way it wasn't odd that I was there for such a long time. Although obviously I was here supporting Sammy. It felt like I was abandoning Robbie. He was still sedated to help his body repair whatever damage had been done, but the doctors had promised to call Shane if anything changed.

As we were leaving, a couple approached us and there was no need for an introduction. By their features it was obvious they were

Robbie's parents. He was the spitten image of his dad. They'd been on their way back from a trip to New York when they'd heard the news. They rushed to Shane who took them to one side and reassured them their son was in good hands. They had missed visiting hours and his mum was a mess. She whispered something to Shane, and he nodded. She looked at me and I suddenly panicked. Did she approve of me, or would his parents think I wasn't worthy of their son? Her face softened as she approached me and grabbed my hands.

'Leah?' she queried. I nodded. 'I'm so pleased to finally meet you. Robbie's told me so much about you.'

I relaxed and squeezed her hands. The tears fell and she embraced me motherly. She asked how I was, but I couldn't answer through the tears. Shane ushered us all to a waiting car and said he would find his own way back. Robbie's parents were quickly booked into a room in the same hotel and we spent the rest of the night together. His dad was very quiet but polite enough. Who could blame him? I was a stranger as far as he was concerned and he was worried about his son. Kathy Hale was only too happy to get to know me.

It got late and I eventually returned to Robbie's room. I climbed into bed, only taking off my shoes. The clean sheets wrapped around me and after a few hours of restlessness I drifted off.

***

Robbie was awake and sitting up, looking much better. The feeling of relief the day before when he had opened his eyes and spoken my name, and with no signs of any lasting damage, had made me realise how much I loved him. It had felt like I'd been holding my breath and could finally breathe again. Even though I had almost certainly lost my job it didn't matter. There was no way I was leaving his side.

Robbie was chatting to his mum,

or rather telling her to stop fussing. He was fine he kept saying. It seemed he would make a full recovery and be back to work in a month after he was given his doctor's permission.

'Son, you're not even out of hospital and you're making plans. You need to rest,' Kathy nagged at her son. Robbie looked at me and rolled his eyes. 'Don't roll your eyes at me, boy. I'm your mother and it's my job to nag you.'

'Yes, Mum.'

Robbie loved his mum but anyone could see she could be a little over the top. I knew she fussed even if he had a cold, so this gave her more reason to worry. Robbie hated her fussing and reminded her he wasn't a child anymore.

'Robbie Hale, you will always be my baby.'

'Oh, for the love of God, mother. I am going to be fine. I'll eat later.'

Kathy was not far off force feeding him. I needed to find a reason for her to leave so he could have a bit of time without her bothering him. I forced a yawn and leaned back in the chair. Kathy was on alert and asked if I was OK.

'I'm so tired. I need more coffee.' It did the trick. Kathy was on a mission for coffees. I knew it was a good ten minutes from the room to the café and it was always busy. She'd be at least thirty minutes on her hunt.

'Thank fuck for that,' Robbie said sounding relieved. 'She's driving me nuts. I love her, but fucking hell she doesn't half go on.' Robbie glanced at me and looked thoughtful. 'You didn't need coffee, did you?'

'I thought you needed some space.' I laughed.

Robbie grabbed my hand and pulled me closer. 'All I want is a kiss. She has no idea that maybe we might want just a few minutes alone.'

I couldn't agree more. His lips pressed against mine and I was so happy he was OK. The fact he hadn't brushed his teeth for days didn't bother me. He was alive and I had to hold back from joining him in bed.

But it would have been most inappropriate.

'So, does this mean you're not leaving me?' he asked as he stared intently into my eyes.

'I guess not. You do need me after all to get back on your feet.'

6

Kasha shut the door then sighed as Sammy kissed her. It was safe behind Robbie's front door; there were no windows. Sammy turned to me and nodded. I opened the curtains and stood to the side. Robbie was lying on the sofa and Kasha went over and hugged him, then kissed his lips briefly. I looked away and gritted my teeth.

The situation was awkward for all of us, but a week had passed since Robbie had been released from hospital and had been absent from the media. The fans and press wanted to know if he was OK, and most important if he was still with Kasha. We had to put on this little show to shut them up. It was a completely calculated slip up. I opened the curtains, by mistake, just so the paparazzi and their long-range cameras could get a sneaky picture. Robbie then put on a act of surprise as he realised pictures were being taken then I played my part and quickly shut the curtains again.

'It's done. Now get the fuck out of my house, Gigi,' Robbie snapped.

Gigi smiled smugly. Robbie's reaction didn't bother her. She had got what she wanted and would gladly leave. 'Kasha, don't forget you're to stay here and leave at nine for your fashion shoot. Make sure you are clearly seen leaving.'

'Yes, you've told me several times in the last hour. I heard you the first time.'

I sniggered at Kasha's changing attitude.

'I'd change the attitude. Then again, the company you choose to keep, it's hardly surprising.' She looked at me and then at Sammy, but not Robbie. Oh no, in Gigi's eyes that was who Kasha should be with. Sammy faked a yawn, unfazed by her comment.

'Kasha's free to end things with me, if she chooses. I don't force her to stay, unlike others,' Sammy said, smirking.

'Are you still here?' Robbie barked at the agent. 'The door is that way.'

Gigi picked up her bag and stormed out. I knew she'd be all smiles as she got outside, making it all seem fine. The fact that every person in the room couldn't stand her didn't seem to have any effect. I guess that was why she was such a good agent, although to me she was more of a heartless bitch.

Robbie patted the empty space next to him and I sat down by him. He was recovering well but still couldn't go back touring for a few weeks.

'Well, that was a complete and utter load of bollocks,' Sammy commented as he and Kasha sat down on the other sofa. 'I guess it's another movie night here.'

Robbie sat up. He looked thoughtful. 'I agree, bullshit. Sorry, mate, I'll sort it, somehow.'

Sammy assured him he didn't blame him. 'We're in this together. I think we could have some fun with it,' Sammy said, looking like he'd just thought of something mischievous. 'I mean, they think they know us. Let's mix it up a bit.'

Robbie was all ears. 'What do you have in mind?'

Sammy pointed out that everyone wanted this perfect image of a perfect couple. They'd never shown anything but what they were told to show. 'Maybe it's time for you and Kasha to make your own rules. Spoil the perfect picture.'

Kasha was on her feet. 'Yes, I so want to have a public row.' Robbie laughed and threw his hands in the air. 'I can't wait to have a fake public fallout with you.'

Robbie suggested they did it right then. Kasha to storm out with Robbie shouting after her. Sammy and I then come to Kasha's rescue and offer to drive her to a nearby hotel which will be pre-booked. I would return via a private road that had not been made public knowledge. There was a road that went through the neighbour's property that had a small walkway into Robbie's back garden. Robbie knew his neighbours very well; an elderly couple who saw him as a kind of grandson. He'd always looked out for them and they in turn respected his privacy and knew about me. They were only too happy to help when Robbie called them. The plan meant we would all have a night alone with our actual partners and set the tongues wagging. I wouldn't be seen returning and I'd get Robbie all to myself.

'Plus, it will piss Gigi off,' Sammy added. 'Kasha returns later and you kiss and make up, blah blah. A press release states it was because Robbie's going crazy due to being ill and not being able to tour. All is fine. Blah blah'

'I love the idea,' I said quickly. 'Get on with this row, come on.'

Sammy looked at me before bursting out laughing.

I felt my cheeks go red as I realised what he thought was on my mind. Only that wasn't on my mind as Robbie wasn't quite well enough. I just wanted some space as we had been surrounded by people so much lately.

Robbie's parents had left just that morning and that was only because Robbie had ordered his mother to go before, they fell out. I could see now how overbearing she could be, but in a loving motherly way. She had left on the condition that she came back in a few days, just to check on him. His dad had literally dragged her out the door. He'd told his son to take it easy and instructed me to ensure he did. So, yes, I selfishly wanted some time with him on our own. I'd make no apologies for it. The image of a life without all this sneaking about was starting to take shape in my mind when Kasha suddenly began shouting.

'I've had enough of this moping about. I'm trying to help!'

'I don't need help, I need space. Bloody hell, woman, you nag me all the time.'

'Fine, sit on your own and sulk like a fucking child. I'm done.' Kasha was trying to hold back a laugh.

Robbie composed himself. 'Go then. Go on…'

'I will.' Kasha grabbed her coat and bag and stormed to the door. She held it open and shouted more back over her shoulder and even managed a few tears. 'This is the thanks I get for being here for you. You're a selfish prick.'

Kasha stormed across the drive and the clicking began. She wiped her tears dramatically.

I counted to ten and then we followed. 'Kasha, babe. Wait,' I shouted. She stopped and turned, putting on a great performance for the photographers. Then she burst into tears and I hugged her tightly. 'It'll be OK, he's just stressed out. I'm sure he didn't mean it.'

Sammy offered her the lift, as planned, talking loudly so every word could be heard. Then we left in Sammy's car, making sure the pack got pictures of Kasha crying. Once we were out of danger, we fell about laughing.

'I'd better text Robbie. I didn't mean to call him a prick. I just got into the moment.'

I couldn't talk because I was laughing so much. It had felt good to play our own little game. Sammy was making a call to a friend who would come and pick me up from the back of the hotel. A car that nobody would be looking out for. It was starting to feel like a spy movie with all these cloak and dagger antics.

An hour later I was in a random car with a stranger heading back to Robbie. Pete, who had known Sammy since school and was one of his closest friends, made small talk. 'So, you're Leah, my mate's fake girlfriend who's really dating Robbie, not Sammy who's really dating Kasha. It's like a movie with you lot.' He assured me our secret was safe as his loyalty to Sammy was important. 'He's a good lad. Known him forever.'

'That's good to know,' I said.

After a thirty-minute drive and more small talk Pete stopped the car in what looked like woodland, to the side of which was a wooden gate. 'Just go through that gate and Henry and Doris will take it from there. Here's my number. If you ever need rescuing just call.'

I tucked the number into my jacket pocket, thanked him and quickly left the car and went through the gate. I was standing in a large garden, or maybe it was a field. It was immaculate. The house, which was more like a mansion and much bigger than Robbie's – and his was big – loomed in front of me.

The patio doors opened and an older lady, maybe in her seventies, waved me forward. 'Leah,' she whispered. I nodded and went to her. She had a round face, warm and kind, and was dressed smartly. It was clearly obvious that she still cared for herself and liked to look good. She had a soft voice and was well spoken. 'Darling, lovely to finally meet you. Come with me. Henry, she's here.'

Her husband appeared, also smartly dressed, and looking ready to go out. He was tall and broad, with a grey beard that reached to his chest. 'Ahhh the lovely Leah, the woman who tamed the rock star. Pleasure to meet you.' He took my hand and kissed it.

'Thank you so much for helping.'

Doris waved the comment away. 'Don't be silly, darling. We're happy to help dear Robbie. We think he's a bit smitten with you.' She laughed and I wondered if she too had a thing for my boyfriend. She led me round the side of the house. 'There you go, just through there and you're in Robbie's Garden.'

I crouched down and gasped as I saw a well-hidden gap. 'Thank you, Doris.'

'Go now before our secret is blown.' She laughed again before leaving me to make my escape, or entry, whatever you want to call it.

A few branches caught my hair as I pushed my way through the small gap then found myself looking at Robbie's patio doors. They opened suddenly and Robbie pulled me inside.

'You took your time,' he whispered in my ear. 'Finally, some fucking peace.' We cuddled up on the sofa and Robbie sighed, a contented sigh. 'This is nice being home with you. No hotel room or tour bus. It's like we're other couples, relaxing at home. Shame I've no energy.'

I kissed him and wrapped the duvet around us. 'I'm happy with just this,' I assured him. We ate popcorn and drank beer as we watched a movie and I worried about my job situation.

'I'm sorry you lost your job. I can't help but feel it was my fault.'

'No, it was mine. I'll find something else. It was time to move on anyway. This wasn't how I planned to leave but my rent's due next week. I hate to ask.' I cringed as I heard myself.

'Sure, I'll pay your rent for a few months. Don't worry about money. If you need anything just ask.' He kissed me on the forehead. 'You could move in with me.'

My heart fluttered and I wanted

to scream yes but held back. 'I want nothing more until I can officially be your girlfriend. It just won't work.'

Robbie nodded. He knew what I meant and accepted it. 'You're right. Fair enough.'

'One day we will walk out of this house together. I want to be able to hold your hand, not Sammy's while wishing it was you.'

Robbie pulled me to him and held me against his chest. 'I can't wait for that,' he whispered.

***

Robbie was back on the stage after taking a month out which had driven him crazy. But now he was fully recovered and ready to rock. They had rescheduled some of the cancelled dates and the boys were bringing the roof down.

I screamed and clapped my hands as they played their routine. Kasha jumped up and down next to me singing every word and seeming much happier. Things with her and Sammy were going well, and it was clear that she was truly happy. I never imagined we would become friends and end up dealing with the same issue. It was nice to have her to talk to. We kept each other calm.

Gigi on the other hand was not my biggest fan. After the fake row, Kasha had been in a lot of trouble. Gigi had torn strips off Kasha and Robbie. Shane had added his thoughts but it was mainly for show.

He had bosses who wanted him to keep things calm and all rosy in the Hale and Woods perfect garden. They were a brand, and many people were making money out of the ridiculous charade. Bloody T-shirts, posters, and even a book had been written about their amazing romance. And now there was talk of a movie. It had gone beyond ridiculous.

When the last song was coming to an end I headed to the toilets. As I was washing my hands the door opened and Gigi walked in and stood next to me. I turned to say hello to be polite, but she put up her hand to stop me.

'Shut up and listen. I don't know what game you're playing, but I'm warning you, stop,' Gigi snapped.
'It isn't me playing games,' I hissed.

'You're no good for Kasha. You're going to ruin her. Was it your crazy idea for her to date Sammy and put on that performance the other week?'

'How is it crazy? They're nuts about each other. They have been for a while,' I said, anger rising in me.

Gigi grimaced. 'She can't be with him. He's not right for her!'

I leaned in, our faces nearly touching. 'You mean he's not good enough. Why not? She's happy. He makes her happy.'

'She's a model, she doesn't date...' Gigi stopped and took a deep breath.

'The bassist, that's what you were going to say. Kasha must date the main guy.' Gigi really was unbelievable 'You're a small-minded, control freak. You don't care about her. You know what, you can go fuck yourself!' The slap Gigi gave me was quick and I stumbled backwards. 'Ouch, you're a psycho.'

'Don't push me, Leah. I swear it will be a mistake. Don't fuck this up. Those two are our perfect couple, the world loves them.'

I rubbed my cheek and grabbed my bag ready to leave. As I passed Gigi she grabbed my arm and pushed me against the wall. 'I mean it. Go home before you ruin everything.' She was blazing with anger.

I shrugged her off and glared back. 'Just so you are reminded, Robbie is not your client. You can stick your threats up your arse. Kasha is my friend, and you don't deserve her. Don't push me, Gigi. I have one last nerve and you're getting on it.'

Gigi sneered as if to make me believe she wasn't scared of me. She was mistaken if she underestimated me. I might not charge out of the box straight away, but eventually I would, and it wasn't pretty. 'I will be Robbie's girlfriend; the public will know one day. That, sweetheart, is a fucking promise.'

I pushed her out of my way and stormed out, slamming the door behind me. Feeling good and full of adrenaline I made my way, smiling, to the dressing room. I opened the door with such force it smashed against the wall. The room went silent and everyone stared at me.

'That bitch is going to push me too far. God help me, I'll wipe that smug grin off her face soon,' I barked while grabbing a beer, yanking the cap off and taking a swig.

'What's she done this time?' Robbie asked. I told him about my little run in and without saying a word he was out of the dressing room tracking her down. We all followed knowing this was going to get heated. Robbie was fuming.

Shane was heading our way and it was obvious from his expression that he sensed there was tension. He grabbed Robbie only to receive a load of obscenities as Robbie continued with his witch hunt.

It didn't take him long to find Gigi. She was at the bar talking to some men in suits. I didn't know them, but they looked important and were clearly something to do with the band. They turned to greet him but took a step back, I guess when they saw how angry he looked. One thing everyone knew was that Robbie was nice when he got respect, but it didn't take much to set him off. Once something pissed him off, he was not one to be messed with. He also didn't care who saw his meltdown.

'You!' he yelled, jabbing a finger in Gigi's face. 'Keep away from Leah. You fucking talk to her or touch her again and I will blow this whole thing. You need to understand one thing...' Gigi tried to respond but Robbie wasn't having it. 'Shut the fuck up. For once you will listen. You are not in charge of me, my band or my girlfriend. You're a controlling vile bitch. Stay the fuck out of my way. I am done with seeing your face.' He grabbed a half empty bottle of wine off the bar and launched it against the wall. 'Stay out of my face.'

One of the men, an older guy, took charge. 'Robbie, you need to calm down. There are press in the room.'

Robbie laughed. 'I couldn't give a flying fuck if the queen was here.' He was seething, and he didn't care who he annoyed.

'Robbie, I mean it. You need to calm down. You're showing yourself up,' the suited guy said. He didn't look pleased.

Robbie glared at him. 'What are you going to do, put me on the naughty step? Stop me from playing, fine. I'll fuck off home. You can tell the fans, the venue, that tomorrow's gig is off. Refund everyone and lose money. I don't give a tiny rat's ass. You're all a bunch of snobby pricks anyway.'

'Robbie!' Shane bellowed. 'Get out and calm the down.'

Robbie looked daggers at his manager before he turned on his heels and stormed out. 'Fuck it' were his last words as he left the room. Everyone stood open mouthed, struck dumb.

Back in the dressing room Robbie paced up and down, still angry. 'Don't say a word,' he warned Shane. 'I'm not having that. She hit her for fuck's sake.'

Shane didn't blame him for being mad, nobody could. But there would need to be damage control, again.

'Put out what you like, I'm past caring. I'm going to get drunk.' He grabbed his coat and stormed from the room.

I looked at Kasha and Sammy. I didn't know what to do. The panic on my face must have been obvious because Kasha followed him. Sammy took my hand, and we did the same followed by Vince and Rich. Shane followed on later, arriving with Annie in tow. They were a casual couple. Shane didn't do relationships and Annie was happy with that.

'Causing trouble, Marley,' Annie said dropping herself dramatically into the seat next to me.

'Slutting it I see, Quinn.'

Annie smiled and nodded. 'I prefer to call it mingling. I only want to hang out with my bestie.'

'Yeah right. Mingling.' I nudged her with my shoulder and giggled. 'How are things with Shane?'

'Casual. I like it,' Annie said. She looked smug. 'No drama, just a good time.' She seemed genuinely fine with the arrangement so who was I to argue.

Robbie seemed to calm down after a few drinks and was back to his usual funny self. The night ended quietly and uneventfully with us doing the usual switch once back at the hotel.

Kasha had ignored all calls from Gigi and was mortified by her agent's behaviour. 'I don't know what's got into her lately. She's always been a bit over the top but she's losing the plot. I can't deal with her.'

I waved it away. 'Not your fault she's a crazy bitch. Will we see you for breakfast?'

'Maybe lunch,' Robbie joked as he wrapped his arm around my shoulders. 'Or dinner. I'll get my people to call your people.' He stumbled a little as the alcohol hit him suddenly then roared at his joke as we headed to his room.

7

The huge burger and mountain of chips had been very much needed and I sat back, full to bursting. With my go-to hangover cure I would feel better soon. The waiter cleared our plates and we ordered coffee. From across the table Robbie winked at me and smiled.

Sammy put his arm around my shoulder, then pulling me close he whispered in my ear. 'To the right, teenager unsupervised with a phone which she hasn't bothered to conceal. I think she has at least three hundred photos by now.'

I nodded and giggled to add to the act, making it look like he had whispered something sweet in my ear. I looked at Robbie and was sure I saw a flicker of anger. It disappeared just as quick, but this was beginning to annoy all of us now. I saw Kasha put her head down and take a deep breath before leaning into Robbie.

She rested her head on his shoulder and he kissed the top of her head. Now it was my turn to feel the burn in my chest, like a vice closing around my heart.

I got up and headed to the ladies' bathroom and locked myself in the cubicle. I fought back the tears, reminding myself that it was all fake. But it was becoming impossible. The instinct to hold his hand, kiss him or just rest my head on his shoulder was hard to ignore. Kasha looked stunning even after a night out and I looked a mess. My hair needed washing and my nails needed a manicure. I felt like a train wreck and wanted to run away from it all.

I took a few minutes to compose myself before returning to the table, only to stop short as I saw the table surrounded by fans. They'd been ambushed. Robbie was chatting to the girls assuring them he was fine, fully recovered, and he was touched that they cared so much. But I could see from afar how unimportant Sammy was to them and wondered if it bothered him. It was all about Robbie, and if it did bother his band mates, they hid it well. Kasha was their other focus, and she did her duty.

I walked slowly back to my seat. It was as if I didn't exist as I had to ask twice for a girl to move to let me sit down. My expression must have given my thoughts away.

'Welcome to my world,' Sammy said, obviously reading my expression. My unasked question was answered: it did bother Sammy. Maybe the Kasha thing impacted on the moment, but we had both seen enough of the Robbie and Kasha show. Kasha held onto Robbie's hand as they chatted to fans, the fake smile plastered on with perfection. I couldn't stomach it and wanted to throw up, or maybe that was my lunch. Either way I needed air.

'Sammy, we need to go. I have that meeting,' I said as breezy as humanly possible. Sammy grabbed my hand and threw some money on the table to cover our part of the bill.

'Call you later, Rob,' Sammy muttered as we left.

Robbie watched as we left, his face showing his unease. He was fully aware of our reason for leaving and I felt a pang of guilt knowing he would be feeling terrible but unable to do anything about it.

Outside, Sammy muttered something under his breath angrily as I followed behind looking at the floor. I had no words to start a conversation, and he knocked my hand away as I tried to take hold. He was besotted with Kasha and was furious, unable to contain it. We reached the hotel without uttering a word to each other.

Once inside his room he turned to me. 'I'm sorry. I didn't mean to take it out on you. I was out of order. But you know, it's not just Kasha, it's him. I know it's not his fault, it is what it is. But I might as well not be there.'

'You hate that Robbie gets all the attention?'

'I don't mean to sound like a child, but there are four of us. We are

Contact Insanity, not The Robbie and Kasha Show.'

I held his hand and pulled him in for a hug. 'I didn't think it bothered you that much.'

Sammy looked at me. He looked sad. 'It didn't until now. I never understood this thing with you and joked about it. Now I know and it fucking sucks. I thought he was being dramatic. How he's done this for so long without losing it is incredible. Don't take this the wrong way, I think you're awesome but having to hold your hand and not Kasha's is killing me. Now I can see it more, how all the focus is on him. I don't think anyone cares about us.'

I assured him no offence was taken and that they were all just as important as each other. 'Do you really want the same pressure?' I asked.

After a few seconds Sammy laughed. 'When you put it like that, fuck, no!' He kissed me on the cheek. 'Thanks for clearing my head.'

'Anytime. If I didn't love Rob so

much I'd have bolted long ago.'

Sammy paced the room as he thought it through. 'What we need to know is how long this contract lasts. I mean it can't be for the rest of their lives. So maybe if we knew when they could get out of it we could have a time frame.'

'You're right. That's what we need to find out.' I felt a sense of relief and couldn't wait for Kasha and Robbie to return to discuss it.

I left Sammy and was sneaking back to Robbie's room to wait. As I walked down the corridor I groaned silently as Gigi appeared. My mood was ruined.

'Leah, have you seen Kasha?' she asked, sounding smug.

She loved rubbing my nose in it. She knew perfectly well where her client was. 'You know she's with Robbie keeping up appearances,' I snapped.

Gigi laughed and pretended to suddenly remember. 'Oh of course, that's right, she's with her boyfriend.'

I didn't show her how annoyed I

was. That would only please her. 'You know, Gigi, it won't last forever. The contract will come to an end one day.'

Gigi seemed to stiffen at my comment as she searched for a comeback.

'What's up, G, no smart-ass comment? Did I touch a nerve? You know full well Robbie won't sign another. Enjoy it while it lasts.' I laughed as I pushed past her, shutting her up for a change felt great. There was no response from her. She just glared as I walked away.

While waiting for Robbie to come back I basked in my own glory. I poured myself a vodka and coke and checked my Twitter for something to do. Since the idea of the contract had come up I felt calmer. If there was a date, that would at least be something to work towards even if it meant waiting another year or so. They had been living this lie for four years now. This would all be over soon I told myself.

As I downed the last of my drink

the door of the room swung open then slammed shut. Robbie's expression was nothing short of fury. 'Did that make you feel better?' Robbie snarled at me. His tone was nothing I had ever heard before.

'What?' I snapped back.

Robbie took a step forward his hands balled into fists, his knuckles white. 'Leaving like that with Sammy.'

I couldn't believe my ears. After everything I had suffered for him, it was now me in the wrong, or so he thought. Nobody spoke to me like crap, not even him, however much I loved him. I stood, defiant, and glared at him. 'Yes, it did.' The comment took Robbie by surprise, and he couldn't respond. It was the time to tell him some home truths.

'You know that feeling you had when I left with your friend, unable to do anything about it? Did it make you feel like shit? Did it hurt your feelings?'

Robbie looked at me and his face softened as my words sunk in. He nodded and unclenched his fists.

'That's how I have felt for months, but I had to suck it up and deal with it. You have two options, Tell the world I'm your girlfriend or man up, Hale. Call me when you've got over your little tantrum. Don't ever talk to me like shit again.'

I grabbed my coat and stormed towards the door. As my hand grabbed the handle I was spun round. Robbie's eyes burned into mine but he said nothing. There was no anger, but desperation and passion as he pushed me against the wall as his lips pressed against mine. He pulled at my clothing and my anger melted into lust and I gave into him.

'I'm sorry,' he breathed into my ear as his hand reached between my legs making me moan. My reaction had in some way turned him on. 'Sorry, I'm being a prick. I hate it.' He rested his head against the wall, his lips warm as they brushed against my ear.

I grabbed his hair, angrily pulling his face to mine so I could see him. 'Welcome to my fucking world, Hale.

What you felt today is how I feel constantly. Don't be that guy. The double standards make my blood boil.'

He nodded. We locked eyes and I felt that pull of desire, love, lust and anger merged into one. We kissed fiercely as he lifted me up, my legs wound around his waist and our argument forgotten. We spoke no more as we were lost in each other, and I could forget in these moments the world he lived in. When we were alone it was just us, Leah and Robbie, man and woman in love. He wasn't a rock star to me but my life, my future. As we lay together later that afternoon, he just stared at me in silence as I dared to dream about us in the future once all the shackles were removed.

'I'll call my lawyer later and get him to check the time frame. I don't know how long, but I'll not sign another. No chance.'

I relaxed and continued dreaming. Robbie smiled as I talked excitedly.

'It'll be nice to live my life the way I want it,' he said as he stroked my cheek. This was the side nobody else had the pleasure of seeing. My real Robbie, just a guy wanting to be happy.

Just as I was feeling like we would be OK, my day turned on its head. Robbie had been checking out his social media accounts when his face dropped, and he frowned. I watched as he reread whatever it was before turning to look at me. My stomach twisted into knots.

'What?' I asked as the dread crept through my body.

Robbie handed me the phone and then jumped up suddenly and punched the wall. 'Fuck!' he yelled. I looked at the screen and my eyes blurred with tears.

"Sammy Kirk furious over claims his girlfriend stalked Robbie Hale before dating him."

It was everywhere, and so were edited pictures of old messages from my stolen phone. They had been made to look like I was insane and had made advances which Robbie had denied. I couldn't believe my eyes. Then the picture that confirmed it was me and Sammy leaving lunch earlier that day. Sammy looking furious and a perfectly timed shot as he had pulled his hand away from mine. Underneath was a short video showing us looking like we were in the middle of a public domestic showdown. It was so cleverly done even I believed it could be a couple arguing if it wasn't me as a star feature.

'Oh, Shit.'

Robbie was seething 'This is now going to turn into a witch hunt. You and Sammy are over. He can't pretend to be with you anymore. He'll be ridiculed.'

I was shocked. 'What about me? The fans will crucify me.' I began to shake as everything shattered around me. 'No matter what happens, I'll be known as the crazy stalker.'

I couldn't stay there. Robbie watched speechless as I threw on my clothes. I could feel us tearing apart at the seams and knew all hope was lost. As I was leaving, I collided with Sammy.

'Leah, are you OK?'

The tears answered his question – there were no words needed. I just shook my head in disbelief and carried on walking, blocking everything out.

At reception I asked for a taxi, and could see from the look the receptionist gave me that she knew who I was. Thankfully, she had to remain professional. Ten minutes later I ran to the taxi making it just before the press could corner me.

'You alright, love?' the driver asked.

'I've been better.' The tone of my reply warned him not to ask me anything else. I gave him the address and the rest of the journey passed in silence.

8

My mum looked stern as I told her everything. Home was the only place I wanted to be and it was time Mum knew the truth.

Once I'd finished the whole story she poured more wine, sucking in her breath as she processed my secret life. Suddenly, she came to life, and was obviously not happy. 'Who the hell does this Gigi think she is?'

After telling her all my story I expected her to be furious with me for keeping it all from her. But I should have known she'd home in on Gigi.

'Cheeky cow.' She cleared her throat and looked at me. 'You're dating Robbie Hale, *the* Robbie Hale?' It had taken a while for the name to sink in. I nodded. 'Well done, honey.' She held my hand gently. 'Do you love him?'

I burst into tears and sobbed 'Yes', then told her how impossible it was now and that I couldn't do it any more.

'Crap, if you both love each other as you say you do, fight back. My daughter has more in her little finger than those trolls. My baby girl doesn't let people walk all over her.'

I reminded her that I was an adult not a baby. It reminded me of Robbie's mum, and I realised that all mums were the same.

'Sweetheart, you will always be my baby.' She smoothed my hair and got up to get another bottle of wine. 'Stay here tonight. We can have a proper catch up and you can switch off that damn phone. Let the trolls get on with their pathetic lives. If you don't read it, it can't hurt you. They'll be tearing some other poor bastard apart by the end of the week.'

I wished I could be like more my mum. She'd always been comfortable in her own skin, never letting other people's opinions bring her down. The only thing that ever broke her was losing my dad in a car accident six years ago. She had kissed him goodbye as they both headed off to work, just like any other day, but he never came home. A drunk driver selfishly took my dad away because they couldn't be bothered to call a cab. It had just been me and her since then. Nobody would ever have her heart like my dad. She'd tried but she wasn't ready to allow another man into her world. Her family of three sisters were all as strong minded as she was. I'd had a lot of help growing up with three aunts who had always been there for me, and my nan who had shaped her girls to be strong and independent.

    It wasn't long before my mum had updated her sisters on my news. I was drained when I'd had finally spoken to each of them and them all telling me what I should do or shouldn't do. Their ultimate advice was to stand my ground and if Robbie was worth it not to give up. How I wished I shared their optimism.

***

Annie walked beside me as we browsed some shops, constantly checking her phone which had been glued to her hand all morning. Three days had passed since my public humiliation, and it seemed to be dying down as was expected. An actress had been caught cheating so it was someone else's turn to be put on trial by the public. The stares and whisperings I could ignore, and as long as they didn't approach me I could deal with it.

Next thing I knew, Annie was yelling at a woman who hadn't stopped staring at us for at least five minutes. The women hurried away looking embarrassed. At Annie's outburst the others stopped staring and I was left alone, for now, at least.

'Have you spoken to Robbie lately?' Annie asked.

I'd spoken to him that morning and had to admit that it hadn't been very nice. It just felt like I was losing him. He was so tied to Kasha, and I wanted to punish him for it. We had said some things that we both regretted and now we weren't talking to each other. I felt utterly shit because of it.

Annie looked sympathetic but bored. 'If it's such an issue then deal with it. Tell him to man up and stop being walked all over,' she said.

It was obvious that Annie was sick of the drama, and she was right. This had to be the first time I had allowed myself to be walked all over. I was angry at Gigi and Robbie, but mostly at myself.

We walked the busy high street window shopping and stopping for coffee, but Annie didn't bring it up again. She knew her comment had hit home and would let it sink in, on my own terms. She had known me long enough to know how to get through to me.

I stared into my empty coffee cup until Annie interrupted my thoughts. 'Penny for them.'

'You're right.' I put my cup down with such a smash it was a wonder it hadn't shattered. 'I'm being weak. I'm letting those bastards win. Robbie loves me and I won't lose him. I'm not letting him go.'

Annie didn't respond as I'd expected. There was no smile or punch of the air, which would have been her usual celebration of sticking it on the man, or woman in this case. Her next comment slightly irritated me.

'I've been wondering lately if it's all worth it. If I'm honest. Let's just book a flight and go away and party and let him chase you.'

I looked at her, confused, but also slightly annoyed.

'Leah, I know that doesn't sound very supportive, but you have to admit he's caused you nothing but bloody trouble.' She shrugged her shoulders. 'Just saying.'

It suddenly dawned on me that her attitude had been off these pasts' few days. 'What's your problem lately?' I snapped.

'My problem is you moping over some guy. It's getting boring.'

Her response had taken me aback. 'Oh, I'm sorry if I'm boring you. Feel free to leave. I stupidly thought my best friend could be counted on to support me.' I grabbed some money out of my purse and threw it on the table. 'I'll call you later if I find something more interesting to talk about.' I got up with such force that the chair banged into the next table. I was furious and needed to leave before I said something that couldn't be taken back.

Annie tried to grab my arm as I stormed past her. 'I'm sorry, Leah, I didn't mean it how it sounded.'

Feeling too angry to discuss it I kept on walking. I was hurting enough, but now my best friend had got bored of me. Maybe I was just feeling sorry for myself, but it had cut deep hearing her say those things. It also bothered me. It was so out of character. Annie had always had my back, no matter what. Even if I was in the wrong, she'd tell me, but ultimately defend me. Best friends forever and all that. I guess you grow up and real life takes over. The bus home took longer but I needed to think, and less time sat in my flat alone was a sensible idea. Feeling too pissed off to talk to her I ignored all her calls and messages.

***

After getting off the bus near my flat, an hour walking round the park cleared my head. Walking always helped me when I had things on my mind. Sticking my earplugs in and fading away to my music was the perfect remedy. When it began to rain heavily, I gave up and went home.

My flat felt cold and there was a breeze somewhere, although I was sure I'd left no windows open. Shivering I grabbed a towel and dried myself then changed into warm dry clothes.

I found the source of the breeze. My bedroom window was wide open, the curtains flapping frantically as the wind picked up. I scolded myself for being so stupid. My flat was on the ground floor so anyone could just have climbed through the window. Thankfully, my valuables were still there, including the pile of notes I'd forgotten to take with me. Fifty pounds would not have been safe if someone had got in.

I shut the window and turned the heating up high then checked the internet for jobs, sending out a few applications in the hope that something would turn up and quick. Hopefully, my recent public humiliation wouldn't go against me as a job was a necessity. I had to be realistic. Even though Robbie promised he would look after me I also had to think ahead not knowing how any of this would end.

With a large mug of hot chocolate and half a bag of marshmallows found in the cupboard I vowed to relax and not worry about anything for an hour at least. I settled down on the sofa and flicked on the TV to catch up on my shows. But I missed the end as I soon fell asleep too exhausted to even fight it.

I woke feeling cold again just like earlier. The breeze had blown the papers off the coffee table and my bedroom door banged against the wall. My window was wide open again. There was no way the wind had done that. My blood ran cold as it became clear someone had been in my flat. I scanned the room and then I saw it. A note in the middle of my bed with the words printed out in large bold writing.

"YOU AND ROBBIE WILL NEVER BE PUBLIC. GIVE IT UP. NO MATTER THE PROMISES IT WON'T LAST."

Tears pricked my eyes as I stared in shock at the note, unable to process it. My stomach lurched and I ran to the bathroom and threw up. I was just composing myself when Robbie called.

'Hi, babe,' I said forcing myself to sound like nothing was wrong. He sounded like he was in a better mood and I wanted it to remain that way. I apologised for being such a bitch.

'I'll let you off just this once,' he said then laughed. 'I understand. Are we friends again?'

I told him about my argument with Annie. 'I don't want to lose you too.'

Robbie assured me I hadn't lost Annie. 'Just call her. She'll be fine.' Although he did agree that it seemed out of character. 'Maybe it just came out wrong and you've been stressed.'

He was right and I knew I needed to clear the air with her. I asked why he was in a better mood.

'I've checked the contract.'

I braced myself for the sentence this contract had set for us.

'One more year. I know it seems like forever, but this time next year we'll be free, babe. Can you wait? I won't sign another one, I promise you that. Kasha has said the same, although that's just between us for now. Can you imagine the fuss her bulldog would make?'

I had mixed feelings. At least I had a timeframe. We could make plans, but it was still twelve months of lies. 'That seems like forever, but I guess we've gone this long. We can at least plan.'

'You're the best. I know this is hard but I'm so glad you understand. A year is nothing and when it's over I promise we'll make up for all the time we've lost. First thing we'll do is go out. Dinner, drinks, dancing. Whatever you want.'

I wanted to moan but didn't see the point anymore. 'You know that's all I want. When people ask me who my boyfriend is I want to talk about you. I don't care about the fame; I just want to exist in your real life.' That was the truth, nothing else mattered. 'I want to take you home to meet my mum.' Just the normal things couples do.

'One year and you can have all of that,' Robbie said and a few minutes later I hung up.

I began to daydream about us in a year's time, smiling despite the disappointment and worry I felt. Butterflies were doing dive-bombs in my stomach at the thoughts of my plans. Suspecting that it was Gigi's doing I tore up the note and binned it. She didn't scare me. The next time I saw her I'd make it very clear it hadn't bothered me.

My next mission was to sort things out with Annie and on the second ring she picked up.

'Leah, oh my god. I'm sorry. I didn't mean it. You know I always have your back. But sometimes it just annoys me how you're treated. You never bore me. Forgive me?'

I couldn't stay angry with her as she seemed so genuine. 'Fine, you're forgiven. I have been stressed lately. No wonder you've had enough.' I told her she only had to listen to me moan for twelve more months.

'That's great news,' she said, but she sounded a bit offhand and not too enthusiastic about it.

'You could sound a bit more pleased for me,' I snapped.

'I am, really. I'm just cranky, time of the month.'

I understood and laughed. She was always more emotional at that time. PMT, I guess. I realised how self-absorbed I'd been of late.

'Robbie doesn't realise how lucky he is to have you.' She sounded genuine. 'I've always got your back. My cramps are bad today. Sorry for being a moody bitch. I'll take some painkillers, and all will be good.'

We decided to ditch the drama and go out, a girls' night out was well overdue, and I owed her. Over a few drinks I told her about the odd note and she agreed with me about creepy Gigi and stayed with me for a few nights. Our fallout was forgotten and she made me feel more positive. Best friends are angels in disguise.

9

Tiredness overcame me as I arrived back at home. The weekend with Robbie after six weeks without him while he toured America had been very welcome. He'd ignored requests to be seen out and about with Kasha and she had been snapped alone sparking rumors of a split. To the press it was odd that they hadn't run into each other's arms since he had been away. He had run into mine. He was due to fly to Japan after a show that night in London.

I was back to job hunting having found nothing despite my efforts. Several interviews had been offered but I still hadn't heard anything back, which told me I hadn't got them. Although Robbie had paid my rent again, not earning my own money was soul destroying. But there was no giving up. I searched online for an hour applying for three more jobs before taking a shower then called my mum for a catch up.

'I see Robbie and Kasha are on the rocks,' Mum said and laughed. 'Shame,' she cackled down the phone. 'If only these idiots knew the truth.'

'I know,' I said smugly. 'I thought they were solid.'

We chatted for half an hour then Mum said she needed to head to the shops.

'I need to restock my wine rack, and I'm all out of chocolate biscuits. Sue's coming over later to have a chat about her latest marriage problems.' I could almost hear Mum's eyes roll. Her best friend could create a drama out of nothing. 'I'm going to need it. I love her but she gives that man hell.' I wished her good luck and hung up.

I hadn't even put my phone down before a text message arrived from a number I didn't know. I stared at the screen and froze as I read then reread the words.

"Don't get ahead of yourself. Your future is all mapped out and Robbie isn't in it. You're such a fool."

I felt like I'd been kicked in the stomach, but anger exploded inside me and I decided that I wasn't going to be bullied. I emailed a screenshot of the message to myself, just in case, then replied "GO FUCK YOURSELF"

Seconds later I regretted it. Anger had got the better of me and I began to panic. There was no answer from Robbie, and I started to think something had happened. I left a message for him to call me straight away. When he did call an hour later, I was in a state.

'Who the fuck is this?' Robbie snapped once I had told him everything. He hung up and I knew he was furious too.

I sent him the screenshot. My head was confused and my heart raced as I wondered if I'd done the right thing. I suddenly had a bad feeling that I'd just made a mistake. I paced the flat with a sick feeling in my stomach while waiting for Robbie to call back and jumped when the door buzzer went. I hesitated for a second before answering.

Relief engulfed me as Robbie's voice filtered through the door. I let him in and collapsed in his arms. 'You have a gig,' I said.

Robbie shrugged. 'I *had* a gig. You know I'm sick of being controlled.' His shoulders slumped as he said something I never thought I would hear. 'I don't want this anymore. I'm done with this shit. Fuck the gig, fuck all of it. If they want me back on stage, they stop telling me how to live my life.'

He meant it. This wasn't just about us. Robbie had become a cash cow, a commodity, and he had had enough.

'I didn't start a band for this. Making music and entertaining people is what I want. I feel like an object that means nothing but how much money I'm worth.'

I stood and watched the love he had for his job, his dream, die. 'I've left the others back at the venue and they're angry with me.'

It must have been a very hard

choice for him to make, to ditch his band mates. How do you explain to fans that the front man has abandoned the gig? I felt flattered that he had done that for me, but also guilty because I didn't want to cause problems within his band. That had never been my intention.

'Are you sure this is a good idea? Don't do anything rash, please. I don't want this to cause trouble.'

Robbie took my hand and kissed it. 'This isn't a rash decision. It's been a long time coming. Today just made me realise how controlled I've become, and it makes me sick. Kasha and I are nothing to these people and I'm not having it.'

He looked at me and told me what had kicked it off. Not only had my mystery texter ruined his mood but the talk of Kasha wearing an engagement ring had reared its head again. Gigi had turned up with a very expensive ring.

'I can't take the lie that far. I told them to shove it. Not just for us. I saw Sammy's face; it hurt him. He won't ever admit it, but he was livid. They want a new album by the end of this year. Well, they won't get shit from me until I start being treated like a human being and you have a bit more respect.'

My stomach flipped. This was heading into a serious situation. Robbie held the material that was needed for the album. He would literally go to war with his management and record label, and I was worried sick. He rummaged inside the bag he'd brought with him and pulled out his notebooks, everything that had lyrics and his ideas for the music. Then he held it up to me, his passion obvious in his eyes.

'They want it, they'd better beg for it. They want to play, I'll play. If I don't get what I want, then I'll go public and risk it all. As of now I am on strike.'

His phone trilled loudly in his pocket, but he ignored it. I felt torn. I supported his decision but couldn't shake off the feeling that this was a big mistake on his part.

***

Frustrated, I shifted from one leg to the other as I waited in line at the shop. Robbie had made himself comfortable in my flat and I had gone for supplies – a pack of beer and a bottle of wine. The elderly lady in front looked shaky on her feet as she slowly counted her money. I didn't normally feel so impatient but with a rock star setting up his own protest in my flat I needed to get back before he did something else crazy.

Finally, it was my turn. I bought several packets of cigarettes as well, paid for it all then set off home. It was only a short walk, and I lit a cigarette. The road was quiet as I stopped to check before crossing so I carried on. A few seconds later there was a squeal of tyres as a car raced round the corner. I walked faster to reach the pavement. The car screeched to a halt and the door was flung open. Gigi jumped out.

'Where the hell is he?' she screamed. 'He can't do this. Everyone is fuming. He just walked out and left everyone at the venue. You know, this is your fault.'

I thought fast. Robbie was in serious trouble, but I still had to protect him. 'My fault? No, this is your fault. Everyone involved in this sham is at fault. You've pushed him too far this time. Engagement ring, notes left in my flat. Well, thanks to you I have no idea where he is.'

Gigi stormed forward. 'Don't lie. You know exactly where he is.'

I shook my head and turned away, but she spun me round. She looked confused. 'Notes? What are you talking about?'

I laughed in her face. 'Creeping into my flat and leaving notes to scare me off. Well, it won't work.'

Gigi took a step back her face was blank. 'Leah, that's serious. It's not me.' She was doing a good job at acting innocent, but I wasn't fooled.

'Whatever. Who else is so keen on me giving this up? I won't, so quit your games. Kasha doesn't need him to bloody hold her hand. She doesn't even want him to. Back off. He left my flat an hour ago. We've fallen out. I told him to go back, and we argued over that and the fucking ring. He stormed out and I don't know where he went.'

Gigi sucked in her breath, but luckily, she believed me. 'Shit. Would you try calling him.'

I agreed and pulled out my phone and prayed he didn't answer. He must have heard my prayer because he didn't, so I left a message.

"Robbie, please call me. I know you're mad. Listen, Gigi is with me and everyone's looking for you. I know we said a few things we shouldn't have. Just call me, or Shane. I'm sorry."

Gigi seemed to calm. 'Would you please let us know if you hear from him,' she asked, and I nodded. 'Thanks,' she said as she returned to her car. But before getting in she turned to look at me. 'It's not me. I can swear on my life. Be careful,

Leah.' She left but had almost convinced me. But it had to be her. It wasn't her normal style, but who else could it be?

I ran home before she changed her mind and came back, slamming the door and double locking it.

'I got your message. Good thinking,' Robbie said as he appeared wearing only a towel. He had been in the shower and my heart did somersaults as I looked at him. We had more important issues to deal with before sex and I erased the urge to jump him right there.

'Are you sure this is a good idea?' I asked with a little part of me hoping he had changed his mind.

His face dropped. 'Yes, and no. I am right in the reason, but maybe abandoning the lads wasn't cool.' Now he was conflicted. He wanted to make a stand but would dropping his band in it achieve anything, he asked me while getting dressed.

I wrapped my arms around his waist and pulled him close. 'You really want to know what I think?'

'I asked, didn't I?' He kissed my lips softly.

'OK, I agree with you. It's all I've ever wanted. Not just about us being together in public but for you to be treated like a human being. I'm worried about the effect it will have on the band. While sticking the finger up to the powers that be seems like a good thing, letting your band down isn't. They become part of the snub and that's not fair. They've been so supportive of us. You can stand your ground off stage but continue to be on it. All this will do is hurt you in the long run and you've worked too hard to throw it away.'

He let go of me and sighed heavily as he looked at his watch. It was just gone eight. If he jumped in a cab, he could make the stage in time. But finding one was the problem. I called Sammy.

'Don't kick off, listen.' I explained to him about Robbie and Sammy told me to stay at the flat while he sorted something.

He didn't sound too angry but

maybe the fact that Robbie had come to his senses had calmed him. 'He's a prize prick. Tell him that, but I'll have it out with him later.'

It wasn't long before Annie appeared at my door. 'Your carriage awaits, Mr. Hale.' Shane had called Annie to help as she was close by and had a car. 'Let's go! We're cutting it fine as it is.'

I was a bit miffed as Annie hadn't been answering my calls over the past few days. Shane had called and she had answered him. I didn't tackle it but decided to call her later. I also noticed she'd didn't even say 'Hi' to me which made me think she was ignoring me.

Robbie kissed me on the forehead as he left and they ran to the car. I paced the flat hoping that he made it. The clock showed 9:15, stage time.

My phone buzzed. "All delivered and now hitting the stage." Annie had finally remembered how to text me. I commented on it with my reply and felt slightly better at her response.

"Sorry, babe, I'll call you later. My

phone was playing up, got it fixed this morning. Love you! X"

Next was a text from Shane. "Thank you! You saved the night. Robbie told me you talked him round. Good girl."

I relaxed by pouring myself a drink then settled down for a boring night in front of the TV. I was halfway through some awful zombie movie when another text arrived from my weird stalker.

"Close call. Good work saving him. Enjoy it while it lasts."

I needed to deal with this cretin or Gigi if it was her. Either way it was getting irritating.

"How about you stop being a coward and face me?" I waited for the reply. It took three minutes.

"Why would I do that?"

I replied again. "Because I don't take orders from a faceless wanker."

The response was a simple "No".

"Go screw yourself Gigi, you're pathetic." I sent back. There was no further response so I carried on watching TV. It was ridiculous. It didn't matter what she tried. Robbie had more people to defend him and pull strings. Everything suddenly felt better. I wasn't going to bow down to it so finished watching the movie and headed to bed to read. I was hardly past the first page before falling asleep.

I woke suddenly. My eyes wouldn't focus and everything was black. As I came to I realised there was something over my eyes. There was pressure on my mouth too. The pressure was so great I couldn't speak or breathe. I tried to move but was pinned down by someone on top of me. Their breathing got closer until it was right by my ear.

'Do not test me. See how easy it is to get to you. I will kill him because I want you. He doesn't deserve you.'

I froze with fear. Then the pressure lessened, and I was free. A pillowcase had been used to cover my face and I screamed as I tore it away. But my attacker had already fled. As I sat shaking, tears streaming down my face, one last order arrived on my phone.

"Don't call the police. Shh"

I knew then that I couldn't beat it. They had got into my flat. The sound of footsteps then someone calling my name made me jump. I still couldn't move even at Robbie's voice. As he came into my bedroom, he must have seen the terror on my face.

'What's wrong?'

I fell apart and sobbed out what had happened while he held me. He was angry but I made him stay and not go looking for them. 'Robbie, just go. This will stop if we stop.'

'No!' he yelled. 'No fucking way. I'll deal with Gigi.'

I took a deep breath and said the words that broke my heart in two. 'I don't think it's Gigi. She doesn't like me, but I'm not convinced she would go this far. It wasn't her voice, although I'm sure whoever it was tried to disguise it.' I wasn't sure who would do this. Nothing made sense to me any more. 'Someone doesn't want me around and for both our sakes we should take a step back.'

Robbie wasn't happy with this but even he could see that things were getting out of control.

'Just don't sign anything and come back to me. When you're free I'll be here waiting,' I told him.

He begged me to reconsider, but I stood my ground for his career as well as my sanity. He had other priorities and they didn't include me. Not for now. I'd never seen Robbie cry, but he was close to it.

'It isn't forever,' I promised.

He looked heartbroken and I guessed I did too. Then he kissed me one last time. 'I've never loved anyone like you,' he said as he was leaving. 'If this keeps you safe, I'll do it. But I will come back. Promise me you'll wait.'

I placed my hand on my heart. 'I promise. You are all I want, but when we can really be together. This is too hard.'

10

The chatter of the busy coffee shop helped to calm my nerves. Kids ran around tables while mums sat chatting. They had a normal life, a family life. They'd go home and cuddle up to their husbands happily. I'd sit at home only dreaming of that luxury. Four weeks had passed. Robbie was in Australia with Kasha, or rather Kasha was out there with Sammy. My last contact with my tormentor had been the morning after we had split. It had simply said

"That wasn't so hard."

Robbie still sent me messages and we kept in touch, but never a phone call. Annie had been great at keeping me sane and today was no different. She had called and wanted to meet up for a coffee as she had a day off work. I checked my watch and then scrolled through Twitter while waiting for her.

She was a few minutes late and

looked stressed when she finally arrived. She sat across from me, looking pale.

'Christ, bad day?' I joked. Annie didn't smile at my joke but stared at me. 'What the hell is wrong with your face?'

She took my hand. 'Babe, you know that I love you. Say if you don't want me to, but Shane has asked me to fly to Australia.'

Now I understood why she looked worried. It was obvious that she wanted to go but didn't want to upset me. 'Wow, that's nice.' I forced it out. 'When?'

She shifted in her seat and crossed her legs. 'Tomorrow.'

I failed to keep the disappointment out of my voice but couldn't help it. 'But we have plans to go to that new club. Girls' night.'

Annie looked torn but I knew she really wanted to go. 'I didn't think it was serious with you two?'

'It isn't. But after Sunday's show they have a few days off and have decided to stay there for a few days. He called me on the way here. He says he wants to see me.'

She went pink. Annie was falling for him. I could see it a mile off and should have seen it coming – slightly older man who could show her some excitement. Shane was a good-looking guy, tall and always dressed nicely. He was often told he look a bit like Ewen MacGregor but with black hair.

I forced a smile. 'You'll have a great time.'

'Oh, babe. You're sure?' she checked. How could I be anything else? I wasn't her keeper and couldn't stop her from going. It was nice that she cared, but I felt isolated from everything I cared about. For me there was a whole year to wait. Every day he told me he missed me and as sweet as it was it hurt too. Annie knew the look on my face, and I could tell she felt sorry for me.

Once enough time had passed, I made my excuses to leave. I had to get home so I could wallow in self-pity without a witness. Feeling happy for Annie was mixed with feeling envy.

'Have a great time. Call me when you're back. Tell Robbie I'm still waiting.'

She nodded and I forced a smile, hugged her tightly and left. I pulled up the hood of my jacket to shield me from the wind then stopped to grab some shopping from the supermarket and went home.

A bottle of wine down and I was checking the time in Australia. It would be early morning, but I didn't care as the wine took over. I needed to see his face, so grabbing my phone I hit face time.

After several rings his face appeared on the screen. His eyes were half open and I had clearly woken him. 'Leah, is everything OK?'

'I miss you and I can't stand it,' I sobbed although knowing I was acting pathetic, just like girls I had mocked for behaving the same. But I couldn't stop myself. 'I feel so alone.'

He sat up and I burned with

desire as his bare chest appeared on the screen. God, he was perfect.

'Get your hot self to the airport with Annie. Fuck it, I miss you too. I'll sort it now.'

I shook my head. No, it just wasn't worth it. I would be put on the shelf after a few days, and we'd be back to square one.

'It's a year, only a year, 'I whispered.

After a few minutes, I knew contacting him had been a mistake. I had just tortured myself because his pleas to fly over were weakening me. Hanging up was harder to do. When his face vanished from my screen like he didn't exist I forced myself to sleep. But switching my mind off wasn't easy.

When I woke next morning feeling delicate, I sat up with a start, suddenly worried that our conversation had been heard and someone would be there. My flat was quiet and sunshine warmed my room. I let out a sigh of relief that everything was fine. Maybe I was getting too paranoid. A long talk with Annie over the phone made me feel better. She let me get everything off my chest and promised me I would be OK. She promised that she'd always be there for me no matter what happened.

Two days later I was out for a run to clear my head, in my own little bubble with music pounding in my ears. Anything that didn't remind me of Robbie was fine, with all Contact Insanity stuff off my playlists. I ran for over an hour and didn't feel like going home. I raced through parks and off beaten tracks until my legs screamed for me to stop.

It was only when hunger got the better of me that I gave up. There was a short cut through the fields behind the flats where Annie lived, and I looked up at her window as I passed. Suddenly, I tripped over and landed face down in mud. Great, ending a good run-in humiliation.

I stood up and brushed myself down. A part of the field that looked like it had been dug up and filled in was the culprit. The field was used by dog walkers all the time, and someone's dog must have had a field day digging this hole. Very hungry now and covered in mud, I headed home. The back road was quiet as my building came into view. As I stopped to take a breath the silence was shattered by the revving of an engine behind me. I only saw the figure for a split second before the pain seared through my head and everything went black as I fell to the ground.

***

I woke up feeling uncomfortable. My eyes felt heavy like lead, but eventually they focused.

'What the hell?' I said out loud. The back of my head was painful, and my hand felt wet with blood as I touched the lump that was forming. The headache hit me full force, so lying back down I waited for it to subside before trying again. Eventually I managed to stand and look around me. There were fields and woodland all around me but the sound of traffic in the distance.

It suddenly dawned on me that whoever had attacked me had left me for dead. I needed to call for help but then my heart skipped a beat. My battery was low and before I had time to dial it died on me. I cursed myself for not charging it fully before my run but was thankful it was still in my pocket. The pain was agonizing, but I was angry as the fire in my belly burned with the will to survive. There was a motorway over to my right. Hopefully someone would stop soon and get me somewhere safe.

11

The traffic continued to pass me, and I must have looked a sight, dressed in running gear with blood pouring down my face like an extra in a zombie movie. I knew it was a long shot. It was a motorway; people couldn't just stop. But hopefully someone would.

It was getting cold, and the wind was picking up. Hoping to get more attention I lay down on the ground and pretended to be unconscious. It was wrong, but with a bash to the head I wasn't thinking straight, and I had good reason.

After what was probably a few minutes I heard a car slowing down near me then a female voice calling out. 'Are you OK? Hello.' Footsteps approached and then there were hands on my wrists, checking for a pulse. 'Can you hear me, love?

I opened my eyes and sat up grabbing the angel who'd stopped to help. The woman was middle aged and dressed smartly. 'Thank you for stopping. I need help...' The words came out in broken sentences as I tried to tell her my story, but in my panic it sounded insane.

'You're safe now, honey,' she said.

I was stunned to hear I was only a few miles from Manchester. That was miles from home. How long had I been out cold to get this far? She told me it was almost eight in the evening.

'I'll call for help,' the woman said.

'No!' I yelled. 'I just need to get to a hotel, anything close by. I need to get to a phone.'

The woman, Maureen, she'd told me her name was, seemed a bit hesitant but eventually agreed to take me somewhere to get sorted out. Once in the car she reached into her bag and pulled out a packet of cigarettes and offered me one. 'You look like you could do with one. Once you've calmed down you can tell me what's happened to you.'

I smoked the cigarette and we drove on in silence.

'Now, who are you and why were you lying at the side of a motorway?'

I decided to start my story from the beginning and Maureen listened without interrupting. She seemed to take it all in and let me finish.

'That is one hell of a story. All over you seeing this Robbie guy.' She shook her head, in disbelief probably, and then she smiled. 'You're not going to stay in some cheap hotel, you'll stay at my house. You can get cleaned up, charge your phone and we can think about what you do next. Unless you want the police called?'

I thought for a moment and made my decision. 'No, I want to find this bastard myself and put a stop to it. Getting the police involved will make it public. I don't want them to know I'm safe.'

***

Maureen handed me a glass of wine after I'd cleaned myself up. She'd given me some clean clothes and an ice pack for the lump on my head then ordered pizza. My phone, which was finally charging, suddenly vibrated. Robbie was frantic as I hadn't been answering his messages. I had to tell him something.

Maureen gave me her phone to call from. 'They won't be listening to my phone.'

She said I was welcome to stay with her as long as I needed. Leaving would be stupid, so feeling safe with her I stayed another night.

Robbie contacted me via Maureen and was keeping up the act of claiming he hadn't heard from me in weeks. I hadn't heard from him that day actually, but I knew he was busy and would ring when he could.

Maureen was looking at her laptop. 'Bloody hell, it's you with that Sammy.'

I raised an eyebrow. 'You checked my story, didn't you?'

She shrugged. 'Do you blame me?'

I couldn't blame her. It did sound a bit nuts.

'He's really dating Kasha?'

'Yep, and now we're all in this fucked up mess together.'

I jumped as there was a loud knock on the door.

Maureen laughed. 'Don't panic, it'll be the pizza.'

It was indeed our dinner. I hadn't eaten properly for days and was ready for it.

'How's the head?' she asked as she passed me a whole pepperoni pizza.

'There's a lump the size of Jupiter but I'm OK, I think.' I took another painkiller and attacked my pizza like it was my last meal. It was about an hour later when the battle truly began. My stalker, attacker, I wasn't sure how to describe them, made contact. Clearly, they had gone back to where they had left me.

"Where are you? You are supposed to be dead."

Maureen went pale as I showed it to her. 'Wow, this is messed up.' She paced the room before turning to look at me grinning. 'You're in control now, Leah.'

Suddenly, it hit me. 'Yes, they have no idea where I am.' My reply was a simple "Fuck You". Then I waited, ready for their obvious reply.

"Don't be silly. I will kill him."

I smiled as I typed "I don't think so. He's not even in the same country. What do you want?"

"YOU" was all they replied.

Maureen tried to take my mind off it but failed. I tried to sleep but spent the night wide awake and had worked myself into such a state that by five in the morning I was throwing up violently.

My phone was vibrating as I returned to my room. It was Robbie, and I dived to answer it.

'Leah, I'm worried about you,' he whispered.

'I'm OK. Don't worry.'

'There's more to this. I don't know what, but something isn't sitting right.'

I asked him to explain, but he claimed it was just a feeling. I knew he was holding back. 'Rob, tell me.'

'I can't without being completely

sure.' He wouldn't tell me anymore but told me to stay safe until he called again.

Another day passed then everything changed.

Annie called around lunchtime, in tears. 'I need to meet you, I'm so sorry but I can't keep this from you. I should have told you before but it wasn't until yesterday, I was sure.'

Annie sounded so upset that I told her where I was, feeling relief at having my best friend back. She told me she wanted to tell me in person and had flown in from Australia that morning. I was worried as the hours dragged while I waited for her to arrive.

#####

Annie sat next to me on the sofa, looking distraught as she searched for the words. I pleaded with her to tell me what was bothering her.

'I don't know where to begin. It's breaking my heart. I wish I'd never gone to Australia. It wasn't the trip I expected. It was shocking. Everything I saw and heard.'

I felt every part of me deflate as I realised, she was about to tell me something about Robbie. The way she was, how upset she was, could only mean she knew it would hurt me. The moment she started to speak I wanted her to stop.

'I overheard Shane on the phone. Robbie and Kasha have slept together. I don't know when, but they don't want you to know. Robbie's acting like he doesn't care. Kasha's different when you're not around. I think you've been used, babe. It's a full-on act. I think those two are closer than we think.'

I couldn't speak or move as she explained that Robbie didn't seem to care about me when I wasn't around. Shane had told her during a very drunken night that I was being set up for publicity, to be a crazy stalker and help promote the band and Kasha. I couldn't believe my ears.

'I'm so sorry. I left as soon as I knew.'

'No, he wouldn't do this to me. He wouldn't. He loves me,' I yelled as my heart broke.

Annie grabbed my hands and held them tight. 'I'm your best friend. Would I say these things if I wasn't sure? I know how much you love him, how you've invested so much of your life in him. I don't want to do this.'

She looked sad at having to do this to me. 'It all makes sense now. Why he wouldn't just shut the whole Kasha thing down. It was all to add drama, and bang, in a few weeks you would be outed as his insane stalker, using Sammy as a way in.'

I was so confused. Why would he need to do this? Then everything I'd endured came back to me and I realised that Annie was right. I was always kept at arms' length unless he wanted me around.

Annie looked like she was holding something back and I pushed her on it. She began to cry. 'Oh Leah, this is such a mess. I can't believe how sucked in we were. I thought Shane might be the one. He's just as much a jerk as Robbie.' She reached into her pocket and pulled out a phone, my old stolen phone. 'This was in Shane's room.'

My hands flew to my mouth. 'It was him.' Annie passed the phone to me. The one thing it did mean was that I didn't have to keep the one Robbie had given me as a gift. I took the new phone and stormed into the kitchen, grabbed a rolling pin and smashed it to pieces. I would get a cheap sim card once I could get to a shop. The old one had been blocked so was useless. I was heartbroken and humiliated, but most of all I was livid.

Annie thought it best if we left, found somewhere to stay to think things through and let Maureen get on with her life. 'We can go to my aunt's caravan in Wales,' she suggested. 'Nobody knows about that, and it will give you time to think.'

I packed up my few things and thanked Maureen.

'You don't have to go. Stay here.

You can think here,' she suggested, but we had intruded enough.

'You've been so kind, but this isn't your problem.'

Maureen sighed. 'It's been the most exciting thing that's happened to me in years, if I'm honest. Not that I'm saying I like seeing you go through this.'

Suddenly, I realised this woman might be lonely, but it still wasn't fair to drag her into my chaos. She packed up some food for us and handed me her number. 'Just in case you need anything else. Please let me know you're OK, Leah.'

I promised to call once I had sorted my life out to stop her worrying. Then we drove to Manchester Piccadilly, leaving Annie's car nearby. Annie thought it best to take the train so we couldn't be followed. I thought it was a bit extreme – it wasn't like we were criminals on the run.

'Someone tried to kill you. I'm not taking any chances. They know my car. So we take the train and it'll take them ages to figure out where we've gone.'

It made sense once she had put it like that. We paid for the tickets with cash and headed to Rhyl in North Wales.

12

The caravan was small but cozy. I curled up on the small sofa and Annie handed me a large mug of hot chocolate. It made me think of family holidays as a kid, and I felt safe, glad at the small space. It felt like I had a protective wall around me and I could think.

'I need to speak to him,' I finally said after several sips of the comforting drink. Hot chocolate and marshmallows had always been the way my mum had calmed me as a kid. Annie always did the same.

'No!' Annie snapped. I glared at her shocked by her sharp reply. 'Sorry, he'll lie and talk you round. I can't watch you used anymore.' She messed with her hair, like she always did when she felt nervous or stressed.

'I have to find out if any of it was real.'

'It wasn't,' Annie snapped. It felt like a slap in the face at hearing the harshness in her voice. 'I heard enough this week. Poor Sammy. He's being made a fool of too.'

I'd not even thought about Sammy in this. 'He doesn't know?'

Annie shook her head. 'He's in the dark as much as you. I thought Robbie was a decent guy. How wrong we were. He's only out for himself. He wants more, he wants to have the world feeling sorry for him. Kasha will be the loyal girlfriend, helping her exposure. It's sickening.'

I loved Annie for her loyalty to me, but something was bugging me. Could someone pretend like Robbie was doing? Was I so blind not to see he was playing me? Why would he need to? If I tried to contact him that would upset Annie, and she'd take it as I didn't believe her. Of course, I did. She had obviously seen or heard something to anger her so much. What if she had misunderstood it? And then it hit me. I had told him to act like nothing was wrong. Could this be his way of protecting me? Annie had gone into best friend mode, God love her, and reacted as only a best friend would. I had to explain it quickly.

'Annie, my god. I need to explain something to you. You've got this wrong.'

Annie threw her phone to the floor. 'You don't believe me?' Her expression was hard, accusing.

'Yes, that you believe you're protecting me, but—'

'No, you want to run back to him.' She jumped up and grabbed her phone. 'Fine, call him. Go on, let him lie to you, fill your head will bullshit and humiliate you.'

I tried to explain, but she wasn't listening. 'Leah, the day I flew back he was in his room with a fan.'

Another punch in the gut. My best friend continued to deliver the blows of Robbie's true self. The one the media would want you to believe. I was struggling to hold on to the Robbie I knew. My best friend wouldn't lie, but deep down something wasn't right with this. You could lie with words, but eyes told you much more. When he had told me he loved me they didn't seem like the words of a liar. You didn't kiss someone like he kissed me without feeling something.

Annie calmed down and sat next to me wrapping her arms around me. 'I'm sorry, I shouldn't have said all those things. I just don't want you to go back to him, to them. I don't understand it either, but I must stop you from getting hurt any more. Look at what's happened to you. You were left for dead, dumped like rubbish all because of him. They were trying to get rid of you so they could feed the lies without you coming forward.' Tears rolled down her face 'It's all my fault.'

Annie blamed herself because she had convinced me to get on that bus.

'It's not your fault. I'm an adult and I chose to date him.'

Annie wiped her eyes and took a deep breath. 'I'm going to the shop to get some supplies. I won't be long.'

I lay down on the sofa on the pretense of having a nap. Annie smiled and left. After a minute had passed, I grabbed my phone and the new sim card. It was pay as you go and would do for now. Robbie's number was still hidden on the piece of paper he had given me on our first night, the back of a set list which I'd folded and put inside my phone case as a keepsake. I had to call Robbie. Annie didn't need to know, at least for now. Disappointment on hearing his answerphone kick in overwhelmed me. I had to speak to him so didn't leave a message but occupied myself with checking my social media. I regretted it immediately. Annie had been right; I was just a pawn in their game. My name was everywhere.

"*Who the hell is Leah fucking Marley?*"

"*As if Robbie Hale would leave Kasha for that Leah chick, have you seen her!*"

"*Leah Marley better stop stalking Kasha's man. Bitch gonna get cut up.*"

"*She is delusional, as if he'd go*

for a plain Jane over Kasha Woods. Girl needs help!"

"Leah Marley is one evil bitch. Trying to take another woman's man."

"Robbie Hale is god. Leah Marley is a nobody. She spends 5 mins on the bus and thinks she's, his girlfriend. How sad is this girl?"

Those were the nicer ones. It was my first experience of a trolling on social media. My account had been tagged thousands of times. Looking at a handful was enough. There were death threats and other vile messages. I logged out and tried to shake it off. I'd always said I would never let a few idiots online bother me. But it wasn't as easy as I had thought.

A picture Annie had taken of us both, laughing together on the tour bus the night we first met the band had been retweeted fifty thousand times. I ran to the bathroom and threw up. My stomach tightened in knots and my world shattered. In that second, I hated him, but it didn't stop me texting him.

"How could you? It was all a lie. I know you've been sleeping with Kasha. I hate you. So, I'm you're stalker? Annie has told me everything. We are done."

I wasn't finished. Next, I sent Sammy a message to tell him what I knew. If my heart was going to be ripped in two, then he was going to go down with me. Causing a rift in the band was one way to get back at him. His band were his life, and I would destroy it. Then I switched off the phone and launched it at the wall.

Annie arrived back to find me howling with despair at my utter stupidity. She scrolled through the abuse, her eyes glistening with tears. 'I hoped I was wrong. The disgusting bastards.'

When I woke next morning, having cried myself to sleep, I felt no better. For now, I would stay hidden. Facing the world was a scary prospect.

13

I waited for Annie to return from getting something for dinner from the little store on the caravan site. She had said the TV in the caravan wasn't working, but I couldn't stand the silence any longer and decided to see if it was fixable. The set was plugged in but switched off at the mains. The caravan was fitted with cable TV and once the power kicked in I was confused to find everything working. Annie must have been mistaken. There wasn't much to choose from so I settled on the news. It was one way of feeling like I wasn't cut off completely from the rest of the world.

I was making a cup of tea when I heard the news reporter and froze at his words:

"Shane Richards, manager of Contact Insanity was found dead in his hotel room two days ago. The police investigation is on-going. The police are looking for Annie Yates, who was believed to have been with him just before his death and possibly the last person to see him alive. The 24-year-old is wanted for questioning."

My whole body was shaking now. No matter what had happened I had to call Robbie. He would be devastated. Annie had been gone longer than expected and as much as I didn't want to think badly of my best friend, I couldn't shake off the feeling she was involved somehow. Her odd behaviour was out of character.

I switched off the TV and grabbed my phone. But just at that moment Annie arrived back with bags full of food and drink, and I jumped.

She laughed, seeming like her old self. 'Chill out, babe.'

I couldn't say anything but just stared at her, studying her face for signs of anything. She was smiling as she handed me a large bag of onion rings, my favorite. I forced a smile as she opened a bottle of wine and we sat making small talk while we refueled or got drunk. Either way I was in turmoil.

'Leah, are you OK?' Annie asked.

'I'm exhausted. I think I'll get some sleep. It's been a hellish few days.'

The lump on my head had shrunk but was still sore. My head was pounding, and I just wanted to switch off. The caravan had one other room and Annie said she was happy to take the sofa. I grabbed my bag of onion rings and went to bed. It wasn't a big room, just big enough for a bed and a wardrobe. I desperately wanted to change into something comfier and grab a shower but had nothing with me. A shopping trip for more clothes was our mission next day. Utterly exhausted and with the pain in my head not easing I just kicked off my shoes and crawled into bed.

A few hours later I woke feeling slightly refreshed and ready to face my problems. I was going to confront Robbie and stop hiding, plus find out that whatever had happened he must be devastated over his manager. My need to find out what had happened was foremost in my mind. Annie needed to know. She clearly didn't know as she would have said something. If it was true about Robbie, I would walk away and put it down to a bad chapter in my life. I've been treated badly before but was still in one piece. This time wouldn't be any different.

I jumped out of bed full of determination and looked for my phone, certain that I had put it on the floor beside the bed. But it wasn't there. After searching the room, I went to get some breakfast assuming that my phone must be in the main part of the caravan.

Annie must have read my thoughts and handed me a strong coffee as soon as she saw me. 'How are you this morning?' she asked.

'Better. I'm putting a stop to this today.' I told her what I was going to do and banked on her support.

She was quiet as I spoke and seemed a little cool. She began to shake her head. 'No. You can't speak to Robbie.'

Her telling me I couldn't speak to him was starting to get annoying. 'I can't ignore this. I have to know what the hell is going on. I'm not staying here like a criminal on the run. I've done nothing wrong.'

The slap was fast and unexpected. I stumbled backwards, dropping my coffee. My legs and feet were soaked, but I was stunned that my best friend had just slapped me.

'What was that for?' I screamed at her. I was shaking with fury. The look she was giving me was chilling and not like the usual Annie, and it scared me.

'Where do you want me to start, Leah?' she demanded. She glared at me; it was a look of pure hatred.

'You can't go anywhere. You are not leaving me.'

I stepped back holding my hands out. 'What?' What do you want? Annie had never given me reason to be frightened of her before, but I was now. She was different.

'You, that's what. Why can't you

just leave it? Why do you always get what you want?'

She was crying, that ugly crying, her face all screwed up. 'All our lives you always got the guy. They never wanted me, always you!'

She began to list all my exes, even from school. It wasn't a long list, but then it all made sense. She had wanted them all, set her sights on them. But they'd wanted me. I never knew. She had never told me. 'Annie, why didn't you tell me this?'

She threw her head back. 'I did. I would say, oh he's nice or do you think he's got a girlfriend, but next minute there you'd be snogging their face off. I let it go. But then, then came the big one. Robbie. I'd been a fan of that band for months. You didn't care but I should have known he'd see you. I tried hard to let it go because I do love you, but it was unbearable. I thought things were looking up with Shane.'

She stopped talking and sobbed. I tried to comfort her, but she pushed me away. The truth was even more shocking. Shane had told her that he didn't think it was going anywhere. He didn't want to be with her, and he was too busy for a relationship. This had broken her heart despite her claiming it was casual.

'Annie, was it you? Did you kill Shane?'

She looked terrified that I knew, and I admitted about the TV. 'I didn't mean to, I swear. I was so angry and hurt over everything he'd done to you and me. We were fighting and he tried to throw me out of his room. I lashed out and pushed him, he fell backwards and hit his head on the edge of the table. I didn't mean it.'

I collapsed to my knees, unable to breathe. 'Oh, Annie, what have you done?' I couldn't get my head around any of this, my only true friend betraying me. 'I'm your best friend. Why?'

'Because you took Robbie, you had to go for him.'

'He chose me, Annie. If you had told me how you felt, I wouldn't have done it. Please listen to me. I'll give him up, but you must stop this. Was all of this you?'

Annie laughed. 'Took you long enough to work it out. I was good, wasn't I?'

I couldn't stop the tears from falling. 'You did this to me?'

'You always got everything. A loving family, friends, boys just seemed to flock around you. Then there was me, good old Annie, she doesn't mind. Well, newsflash – I do.'

Annie had never had a very close family. Her dad had disappeared once her mother fell pregnant, never to be seen again. Her mum did her best but didn't cope well on her own and Annie had been sent to live with her grandmother until she was eighteen. Her relationship with her mother had never really been healed. Annie was a lonely person, and I hadn't seen it. She'd masked her misery with fake confidence and the cracks were now showing. Shane had been her last straw.

'You need help, Annie. I'll help you; I promise.'

She grabbed my hair and dragged me to the bedroom, then punched me causing me to fall to the floor. Then she used some old shoelaces to tie my feet and hands together. After taping up my mouth she paced the room muttering to herself.

'I just wanted something of my own. I've never had anything, I thought you would be the one thing I could rely on. Robbie ruined that by picking you and trying to take you away.'

I looked at her pleadingly hoping for her to remember who I was. Was my best friend still in there somewhere? That fact she had turned on me was hurtful, but she was clearly in pain, mentally. I should be mad, hate her even, but I couldn't. I wanted to help her, to prove my love for her. But she wouldn't look me in the eyes and a few seconds later she left

14

The struggle with my restraints was painful as the laces dug in and I crawled as well as I could to the door then lifted myself up by pushing myself against the wall. I used my elbows to push the door handle down but lost my balance and fell through but managed to drag myself to the kitchen area. There wasn't much to choose from as the caravan wasn't kitted out for habitation. Annie's aunt hadn't been there in months and was preparing to sell it. A couple of blunt knives and forks and a can opener were all the cutlery drawers had to offer me. I lay down on the floor trying to stop the panic, feeling like everything was against me and needing to think.

The time passed as silence engulfed the small space and the only sound was my breathing. Then it struck me – the gas hobs. I would burn my ties off. I struggled to my knees and using the cupboard handle pulled myself up. The four hobs were my only hope. Using my tied hands to turn the knob to release the gas and my chin to press down on the igniter I prayed it would work.

The clicking as the gas tried to ignite was deafening. It wouldn't light at first, but I kept trying till it finally lit and I cried with joy as a small flame edged around the gas ring. It was enough. It was going to hurt so I took a deep breath then held my wrists over the flame. The lace smoked and I gritted my teeth as my skin began to sting. Then the flames took hold and the lace started to disintegrate. Pulling hard to try to remove it I moved quickly to the sink to run water on my skin as the lace burned around my wrists. Then it gave way completely and I was free.

I turned on the cold water and let it cool my skin, feeling sick from the pain. My wrists were burnt but there was no time to dwell on it. I untied my ankles and grabbed my bag, taking one last look for my phone, which I eventually found in the bin.

The sound of messages hitting my inbox was constant. Seventeen, plus five voice messages. I read the first few from Robbie.

"Annie, I know you have this phone. I know what you've done. I know everything. Where is Leah!"

"Annie, Leah is your friend. Don't hurt her please."

"Leah if by any chance you see this, I love you. Everything Annie says is a lie. She killed Shane because he was going to tell you."

Then the penny dropped. Annie had told me a pack of lies, Robbie hadn't done the things she'd claimed. She didn't want me to contact him because she'd be exposed. I didn't hesitate to call him and burst into tears as soon as I heard his voice.

'Leah, thank fuck. Are you OK?'

'I want to curl up and cry. I don't understand any of this. She said she's going to kill me. What has happened to my best friend?'

Robbie told me he was sending an Uber to the caravan park, and it would take me to a nearby hotel.

Once I was safely there, he would come to me. He had flown back from Australia, their tour cancelled after Shane's death.

I left the caravan and headed to the reception area where the car would pick me up and hid behind a huge plant while looking out for my ride out of there. Then I saw Annie heading back to the caravan and froze, hoping she didn't look my way. Thankfully she didn't, but she looked annoyed. Her plan obviously wasn't going well. I needed the cab to hurry up before she reached the caravan. She turned and then was out of sight, but in a few minutes, she'd know I was gone and come looking.

I saw the Uber coming and darted towards it. The driver could clearly see I was distressed but believed my story of a family emergency and that we needed to hurry. As we headed away, I could finally breathe.

The hotel wasn't far away and having checked in I waited for my knight to come and save me. Reflecting on the past few months made me realise how easy it had been for Annie to be my tormentor. No way had she been under suspicion. And nobody had been watching me because I told her everything. I felt numb, wondering how to process this betrayal. I couldn't break my bond with her as half of me was angry, but the other half was worried for her. The door suddenly opened, startling me. Expecting it to be Robbie, I froze as Annie entered the room. Now I was trapped.

'You shouldn't have done that,' she hissed as she stared at me coldly.

I heard a voice outside the door asking if all was OK. Annie turned, popped her head round the door and replied, 'Yes, thank you so much. My friend will be fine now I have her medication. You've been an angel.'

Annie had used the ill friend trick to access my room, using a kind-hearted cleaner to let her in. She closed the door and spun round fiercely. 'You should not have run. I was going to explain everything when

I got back.'

'Robbie's explained everything to me. You lied, you killed Shane in cold blood,' I snapped back. 'Annie, it's over.'

Annie just laughed and moved towards me. 'I've only just begun. People always think they can out smart me, but they can't, although many have tried.' She laughed again but seemed to be in another world. Once she focused back on me, she pulled a large knife from her pocket. 'I'll make it quick.'

She lunged at my face with the knife, but I ducked and with all my force charged at her. We struggled until she overpowered me, sitting on my chest, the blade nearly touching my throat. I focused on the knife, my heart beating so much I thought it would explode. Sweat ran down the back of my neck as she glared at me. That was when I noticed Annie didn't seem right. Apart from the psycho act, which was out of character to start with, there was something else. I didn't know what was bothering me but my instincts were screaming inside.

Time slowed down as she prepared to kill me. It was when she raised her arms, a broad grin of delight on her face, that it hit me, staring me in the face. This wasn't my best friend. It looked like Annie, sounded like Annie, but it wasn't her.

'Where's Annie?' I screamed. It stopped her in her tracks and gave me a small chance to push her off me.

'What are you talking about?'

'You're not Annie. Who are you?'

'I think the bang on your head was harder than we first thought. Jesus, Leah, I know you're pissed with me but that's a bit far.'

I knew this couldn't have been all it seemed. Annie would never do this to me. 'What's happened to your scar?'

The impostor stared at her arm. Unless there had been a miracle scars from serious burns didn't just disappear. Unlike Annie this person had no scars. And seeing her up closely she also had slightly different coloured eyes. Only a shade darker but enough to alert my subconscious. That was what had bothered me a minute earlier.

'Who are you?'

The game was up and this person knew it.

'OK, fine you've got me. I'm not Annie, but I'm her twin sister. Identical twin sister.'

That made sense although I didn't even know Annie had a sister.

'Oh, don't look so confused. Annie didn't know about me till a few weeks ago. That's when I decided to take over her life. You see, Mummy couldn't cope with twins, and she gave me up. Annie was kept and I hated her. I was pleased to find out it hadn't all been so rosy for her in the end. Then I saw how she was landing on her feet, a loyal best friend, famous friends, and I wanted that. My name's Hayley, or it was. You can call me Annie.'

I still didn't understand how me, and Robbie fitted into this. I grabbed a bottle of water that was on the table next to me. My throat was dry and beginning to hurt. The cold water soothed it. 'What did I do to you?'

'Nothing. I just saw your situation to keep you as my friend. I created it so you would confide in me, like Annie. The worse things got the closer I got to you. Annie's old diaries helped me to become her. It's how I knew about all the times guys had rejected her for you.'

Hayley confirmed that everything about Annie and old boyfriends was true. 'I shouldn't worry, she forgave you. I just made up all the hate from her. You see, she was sad in one way, but you were happy, so she got over it.'

I asked if it was the same for Robbie. Hayley shrugged. 'I'm not sure. She'd started an entry about the night you met him, but for whatever reason she never finished it. It just said that she guessed it was always going to happen, that Robbie would like you and she was used to it now.' She shrugged again. 'She loved you like a sister. That wasn't an issue. And once Shane came on the scene, she seemed happy, according to her diaries. She fell for him bad. I think she got over whatever she felt for good old Robbie.' She leaned forward and whispered, 'You don't have to feel guilty for the rest of your life for that. I'll give you that.'

Now, I felt worse, and I couldn't even talk to Annie about it. I wanted more than anything to tell her I never meant to hurt her. I just never knew. 'Where is she?' I hissed.

'It doesn't matter anymore. You won't be around much longer to worry about it.' She sounded like she was getting very bored. 'Enough chit chat. I've decided if we die together it will look like a suicide pact. I've already written our final notes.' She pulled two envelopes from her jeans pocket.

'You're actually insane.'

'No. I'm not. I just can't be bothered any more. Prison isn't where I want to end up. I've no option but to die with you. It's beautiful, don't you think? Best friends together forever.' She let out a sinister laugh. 'I'll be innocent considering nobody knows about me. By the way, I left a note to implicate Annie, just enough to stop anyone looking for me. Hayley never existed and she never will.'

This wasn't about Robbie at all. Hayley wanted me, a best friend, and she'd kill us both to stay together.

'What did you do to Annie?' Feeling sick, I waited for her response.

'She's gone.'

My entire being felt like it was shattering. 'You mean she's...' I couldn't say the words.

'Dead. Yep, it's perfect. Nobody is even looking for her. They think I'm her. It's why I had to get rid of Shane. He started asking too many questions. He caught me without the burn mark and my real passport, and I had to shut him up. You see he liked her, noticed everything about her, that's why the trip to Australia. He'd decided to settle down. So at least they're together now.'

Hayley carried on talking, mostly delusional plans that were never going to happen, but I had to let her think she was in control.

'How did you find me here?' It was something that had just occurred to me.

'You think I didn't see you hiding behind that plant then the Uber turning up. There was a car sat beside reception, engine still running as they went to check in. It still had the owner's luggage in.' She giggled at that. 'Well, I guess it's time to complete the plan. You've nearly finished the water. That was easy.'

I looked at the bottle. 'What did you do to the water?'

She tilted her head and smiled at me, a malicious smile. 'Don't worry, just some sleeping pills, lots of them. I planned just in case I needed to shut you up. I'll let you get some rest before we die together.'

Hayley moved quickly and held the knife to my throat. 'Time for a nap, so be a good girl.'

I did what she told me even though I could feel the pills kicking in. The thought of being under her control terrified me. She held the blade across my throat as my head sunk into the pillow. 'It will all be over soon, bestie.' My eyes started to close, and I tried to fight the sleep. Then I heard the door and a shout. The blade was whipped away, and I struggled to open my eyes as Hayley was dragged away.

'Leah!' Robbie's face appeared above me and he pulled me into his arms. 'I've got you now.'

There was commotion going on all around us but nothing mattered any more. Hayley's screams as she was dragged out by police faded into the background and I was back where I belonged.

15

We had said goodbye to Shane. I walked behind Robbie as we left the funeral with Kasha by his side playing the doting girlfriend. Sammy walked beside me as we played the ex-couple united in grief. It made me sick.

Robbie kept a brave face in public, but I had heard him cry when he thought no one could hear him. Shane had always been there for him no matter what, always had the band's back. He'd be sorely missed. They had a new management team in place and after a few weeks off it would be business as usual. Shane would want that, Robbie had said.

We headed to a private gathering for family and close friends only and spent a few hours remembering the man who'd been a big part in the band's lives. Robbie was quiet for most of the day, and I did my best to get through it without crying.

Annie was still missing, and

Hayley refused to talk about her. I knew that something awful had happened but couldn't bring myself to accept that she wasn't coming back. I hung on to a tiny thread of hope. Three weeks had passed since Hayley had been found out. She was claiming insanity, but several doctors had declared her sane, just very cunning and bitter.

It was getting late in the evening and Robbie grabbed my hand and pulled me into a private room. 'I promised you I would fix us, that we would be together, and you wouldn't have to hide. So far, I've failed. Today has cleared my mind. I'm so sorry. Once I've dealt with losing a good friend, I'll work on us.'

I touched his face gently and nodded. 'Take as long as you like,' I said. He kissed me but said nothing.

We said our goodbyes and left to hide out in his house. A week passed and we hardly left the house. Kasha turned up as planned but would spend the entire time on the phone to Sammy. If I wasn't with Robbie, I was with my mum or aunts who were just as upset over Annie. Every day seemed so long. It had got to a point where I just wanted to know where she was. Deep down I knew she was dead, but knowing she was somewhere all alone broke my heart.

The days went on and still nothing. I felt empty and useless, and that I was letting her down. There were posters, social media posts and news appeals on TV. We had done everything, and nothing had turned up. Her mother had given me a key and I went to her flat several times a week just in case she came home. She might not have been the best mother, but she was a mess too, heartbroken. She loved her daughter and didn't know where to turn. Today was one of those days I spent in Annie's flat, keeping it tidy and waiting.

Robbie held me tight as we stood in her living room. 'I'm so sorry, Leah,' he whispered. 'She meant so much to you.' Then he kissed my cheek.

I sobbed as he held me against his chest. 'She's gone, Robbie, she's gone,' I wailed.

Robbie couldn't tell me it was OK. He knew what I did. Annie wouldn't have stayed away so long. It wasn't her style.

'I just want to find her. Say goodbye. I don't want her to be alone.'

Robbie soothed me as best he could, but as we stood in her flat we both knew. Her presence wasn't there. I had felt the connection we had as friends severed since Hayley. The guilt ate away at me that I hadn't seen it. She had been pretending to be Annie for weeks, meaning that Annie had been alone, forgotten, and nobody had even known.

The day ended the same. In disappointment.

Another week came and went. Robbie was getting back to work with a few local gigs to get them started. I stood at the back, watching proudly, but my heart and head were elsewhere. I looked at my phone halfway through the set and saw my mum had been trying to call me. Several missed calls and a voice message. My heart hammered in my chest as I ran outside.

My mum's voice sounded shaky. "Call me honey, straight away."

The sounds of the ring tone were terrifying as I waited. Then my world crumpled around me. I buckled at the knees and screamed as my mother told me my best friend had been found dead. I couldn't call Robbie but called Kasha who came running out to me. She held me tightly while my world fell apart again. Then her security team helped me inside before the world and his dog stuck their noses in.

By the time Robbie came off stage Kasha had managed to calm me but I was still a complete mess. Even Gigi had been kind. She'd handed me tissues and made me drink some tea and hugged me. She'd even met Robbie and told him before he saw me that I needed him. She didn't get in the way, but this time kept out of it.

Robbie raced into the room, and I cried again, needing him more than ever now. 'I'm so sorry. I hoped this wouldn't happen. Where did they find her?'

I couldn't say the words, not again, and Kasha spoke for me.

'She was found in the field behind her flat. She's been there for weeks. Hayley's been playing Annie for longer than we thought. She'd stabbed her in the throat.'

'I'm so sorry, Annie, I didn't know...' The reality hit me all over again like a train and I screamed. The disturbed bit of the field behind her flats that had caused me to trip during my run had been her grave. While standing looking out onto that field, hoping and praying she'd come home, all the time she was right there. I had walked right over her. That will live with me forever.

'Get me a car. I'm taking Leah home to her family.' Gigi started to speak but Robbie spun around. 'Don't say a word. I don't give a flying fuck who sees us. Tonight, I'm taking care of Leah. She's needed me before and I couldn't be there for her. This time I'm not leaving her.'

Gigi spoke calmly. 'Robbie, I had no doubt that would be the case. I just wanted to say, you can take my car. As you go out just walk with Kasha and once in the car you can do what you like.'

Robbie thanked her for the offer, but he wanted our own car. We walked towards the back entrance of the venue where a crowd had gathered. Fans and paparazzi. I hung back as Robbie and Kasha left first. They were halfway to the car when Robbie stopped and looked at Kasha, who seemed to have the same look on her face. They looked at the crowd of people and then back at Sammy and me. The flashes and excited shouts engulfed us.

Robbie dropped Kasha's hand and walked towards me. He cupped my face in his hands and kissed me. A passionate, loving kiss that told me I would be OK. He was with me, and we would both get each other through this sad time. A kiss in public, something I had dreamed about. He'd kept his promise but had delivered earlier than expected. Kasha ran to Sammy, and they did the same, sending a shockwave around the country.

'You are no longer the girl at the back,' he whispered in my ear. 'You're right at the front with me, where you belong. If people don't like it, tough. I'm not living a lie anymore. Annie would want you to be happy, so I'll make sure you are on her behalf.'

It was a light in my darkest time. I held onto him, sobbing as the pain over Annie cut me to pieces inside. The confusion around us didn't enter my thoughts, and I didn't care. My friend was dead, but my boyfriend had me. He'd caught me when I was falling. He had kept his promise and when I had needed it the most, he'd defied everyone, risked everything for me. He had been worth the gamble. 'Come on, let's get out of here.'

Kasha grabbed my hand and pulled me into a tight hug. 'I know I'll never replace Annie, but you've always got me. I'm so sorry, and I'm here if you need anything.'

I hugged her back. 'Nobody will ever match up to Annie but you're a dear friend. I'm glad you're finally free.'

Kasha was crying as she let go of me and pushed me back to Robbie.

'Go, before these bastards swallow you up,' Sammy said as he wrapped his arms around Kasha and nodded. 'Go,' he mouthed. 'We'll handle this lot.'

Robbie patted him on the shoulder, grabbed my hand and we bolted for the car. Security flanked us until we were safely on our way.

***

The months passed and I moved in with Robbie. His home was now mine, ours. Annie was always there in my mind. Hayley was about to stand trial for her murder along with

Shane's, and she could rot for I cared. The world had got over the shock of Robbie and Kasha breaking up and moving on. We thought about telling the whole truth, but in the end, we just couldn't be bothered. The story went like this. Robbie and Kasha had drifted apart and found new relationships. I was never his stalker, that was a complete lie. Robbie had given his blessing for Sammy to date Kasha, and he couldn't be happier for his friend, blah blah.

The world is a fickle place because now I was the new Kasha. Robbie and I were perfect for each other. I had my own followers, and some even said they preferred me to Kasha. The threat of any comeback regarding contracts had quickly disappeared. Getting rid of a money-making top band wasn't good business.

Gigi had even seen the benefits of having a happy client and had backed off. Surprisingly, things between us were better. We weren't exactly friends, but we were no longer enemies. She wasn't as bad as I first thought. We had all been sucked into a web of lies and she had just been doing her job. She'd been trying to protect her client and her reputation, but even she had seen the error of her ways.

Now Kasha didn't feel so suffocated she had begun to love her career again. She had cut the fake friends from her life. I was seen with her now. Annie would always be my best friend, but Kasha was doing a good job at filling the gap she had left. Annie had somehow in her death healed the cracks in us all.

I'd like to say that I had finally got what I wanted, which was true, but losing my best friend hadn't been in the plans. She would be my strength and her attitude would be my attitude from now on take what is yours and hold on for dear life. My advice for anyone is that things are never straightforward, but if you want something fight for it. Even if you risk losing something along the way.

Annie and Shane paid the price but knowing that somewhere they are together gives me peace. Contact Insanity were celebrating a second week at number one in the charts with their single 'Missed' dedicated to them. Robbie had written the song days after Annie's funeral, and it had been a hit from the moment it was on the radio. The world only knew half the truth with a few red herrings to keep some of our privacy. Hayley was seeking revenge for her mother giving her up. Annie and Shane had been the sacrifice.

The world is a harsh place. It will kick you when you're down, but you should always get back up. Don't be like the old me, the girl at the back. Take a step forward and be the girl at the front with your head held high

ABOUT THE AUTHOR

Kat Green was born Nov 1979 into a military family and moved around a lot during her childhood. This shaped her into the person she is today. She is at ease with meeting new people and adapting to new surroundings. Her family roots are from Stoke-on-Trent, Staffordshire. Kat now lives with her husband and son on the south coast of England, Portsmouth. She doesn't pretend to be the best and is still growing as a writer. She loves books and has a busy imagination. Her love for music plays a big part in her first series.

Kat can usually be found at gigs around the UK finding new music to blog about. Her writing began in 2010 after the sudden loss of her mother to blood cancer.

This made her look at life in different way, life is short, and tomorrow is not promised. It was time to put her stories on a page and be brave.

More works by Kat Green

Strings (The Black Eagles Series Book 1)

Encore (The Black Eagles Series Book 2)

Finale (The Black Eagles Series Book 3)

Veiled

Frozen Pact

Listen To me

Surviving The Game

Follow on Social Media

Bookbub   http://bit.ly/2Wiu4g9
Facebook http://bit.ly/2WCvkKJ
Twitter   http://bit.ly/2wAGRvm
Instagram http://bit.ly/2Z3Xls2

Printed in Great Britain
by Amazon